BEACH
SPACE

Lee Ducote

Raccoon Bend Publishing, Benton La.

Beach Space

Lee DuCote
Copyright © 2017 Lee DuCote.
Raccoon Bend Publications
Benton, Louisiana

ISBN-13: 978-0-9966432-7-6

In Publication Data
DuCote, Lee

Printed in the United States

Dedicated:

This series is dedicated
to my first love...
my mother.

Also by Lee DuCote

Fields of Alicia
Waterproof
Across Borders
Micah: The Sword of Malachi
Camp 80

Chapter 1

Cedar Branch had a long-standing rule about BBQ grills on the balconies of The Tower apartments, a rule created by an incident five years prior to Jack Goslin moving in. On the sixth floor facing the tranquil emerald gulf, a retired couple was enjoying the evening cooking chicken on a newly acquired stainless steel grill. The gentleman opened the lid to inspect the meat, and their curious two-year-old Persian cat leaped on the grill, catching the hair of its tail on fire. At the same time the cat suddenly combusted, the lady opened the door to the balcony, allowing the fire ball to run inside, catching the curtains, couch, a vase of silk flowers, and unpaid tax documents on the table on fire. After an hour of extinguishing the flames, the couple was left with ruined furniture, burnt chicken, unreadable taxes, and a bald cat—thus generating almost instantly the "No BBQ grill" rule.

In the midst of a welcome cool front, though, the residents of CBC were out enjoying an evening without the brutal heat that the South was so notorious for developing. On the fifth floor of the Tower apartments, Karl lifted the top off the grill to inspect the filets wrapped with bacon slowly cooking on Jack's new grill. Picking up a pair of cooking tongs, he gently lifted one of the pieces of meat and examined the bottom. "You keep opening the top, they'll never get done," Jack said, walking back out on his balcony with a refilled glass of bourbon.

"Your fire is too hot! They're gonna burn," Karl groaned.

"If you're looking, then you're not cooking! The fire is fine."

Karl mumbled a few words, then made it over to the rocking chair he had claimed weeks earlier when Jack moved in. The sound of the construction work from below started to die down as the time neared 6:00 p.m. and quitting time. Jack leaned over the railing and watched a few young men roll up a couple of orange extension cords while others locked down their tool boxes and work areas. Pulling his attention back to the grill, he saw Karl lifting the lid again.

"You are as nosey as the Stevens Sisters."

Karl closed the lid with an indignant "I am not! Your fire is too hot." Pouting, he made his way back to his rocking chair.

Jack sat down next to him. "You are like the wife I never had," he chuckled while taking a sip from his 1792 Ridgemont Reserve bourbon.

"Huh. You drink too damn much to be married to me," Karl said under his breath.

"I'd drink more if we were married," Jack answered even more quietly.

"What?" Karl asked.

"Nothing."

A commotion broke out under their balcony, causing both men to exit their chairs and lean over the railing in time to see half a dozen construction workers standing below the third balcony with arms outstretched to catch the cold beer cans being tossed down. The Stevens Sisters had moved from one side of the apartments to the other, giving them a front row to the Gulf of Mexico. "Hey, Rutherfurd!" Violet looked up, yelling at the two older men, "you on fire up there, or did you finally decide to burn that painting you made last week?"

Karl rolled his eyes. "Good Lord! It's like Mardi Gras meets redneck central around here!"

The six construction workers cheered and waved to the Stevens Sisters as they made their way to their trucks with half-a-dozen cold beers. Beyond the construction and across the highway, the waves crashed on the white sandy beaches of southern Alabama, occupied at this end of the day by only a few people taking their strolls and awaiting the sunset.

"Hey Goslin! You want a beer?" Violet shouted up toward the two men.

"Just poured a glass," Jack held out his bourbon. "Do you want some Mardi Gras beads?" he shouted back, looking at Karl and adding to his earlier comment.

"Hell, yea!" Violet shouted back and grabbed the bottom of her shirt to pull up, knowing what it meant to ask for beads on a parade route during Mardi Gras.

June grabbed her hand, "Violet, nobody wants to see your girls. Jack probably doesn't have any beads."

"Yea, you're probably right. Plus who am I kidding—there's no way in hell they would be able to see the girls from above me, they've been hanging around my waist for fifteen years!" Violet walked back into their apartment.

The men settled back in the rocking chairs awaiting the filets and an evening that promised a colorful sunset. "Well, I'll hand it to those workers; they finished the bridge in record time," Jack said, pointing at the new bridge that crossed the highway from CBC to the beach. "It's only one lane. And now that we can have golf carts, it's just going to cause a traffic jam to get to and from the beach!" Karl griped.

"Are you and Betty going to buy that four-seater?" Jack asked.

"Now why in the hell would I buy a four-seater golf cart? I'm not running a taxi service."

"In case I need a ride."

"Drive your own damn golf cart."

Jack laughed at his comment as a strong knock came from his door. "Betty?" Jack asked.

"No, she's down at the art center with Kat."

Jack walked through his apartment and set his glass down on the counter top before opening the door. "Jack, you know the rules," Derrick said, leaning on the door frame as Jack opened the door.

"I've got you a steak on the grill, had them flown in from New York," Jack replied, stepping out of the way to allow Derrick to walk in.

"Cooking me a steak is not going to undo the rules." "Maybe for tonight; I'll get rid of it tomorrow."

Derrick followed Jack to the balcony, adding a "Hello, Mr. Rutherfurd."

"Have you bought that girl a ring yet?" Jack asked.

"Not yet."

Something caught Jack's eyes beyond the conversation, and as he focused on what was flying from the Tower Apartments, a loud explosion echoed from below, and the object flying out from the building disappeared in an orange dust cloud. Karl spit out his drink. "Good Lord, what in the hell was that?"

A voice shouted from below them, "Pull!"

The three men witnessed another clay target leave the Stevens sisters' balcony, followed by another explosion from the shotgun barrel following its clay target. People on the beach ran for cover, a man riding his bicycle ran into a sign, and a flock of sea gulls scattered for their lives. "Pull!" Violet shouted again, followed by another shotgun blast.

"Keep my steak warm—I'll be right back," Derrick said, dashing out of Jack's apartment on his way to the third floor.

"I swear, those damn hillbillies will be the death of us!" Karl grumbled, holding his chest.

Chapter 2

Betty gave Kat, who was giving her art lessons, no time to ask questions after hearing the two explosions, but instead bolted from her easel out the door. Kat was left holding her palette, thinking that was the fastest she had seen Betty move since meeting her months earlier on their orientation trip.

"Oh, Dear Lord!" Betty prayed out loud, running toward the Tower Apartments. She had left Karl and Jack alone assembling Jack's new grill with a full bottle of propane, and she questioned their ability to install it correctly. Now all she could think of was the two old geezers being catapulted from their balcony and floating in the Gulf no closer than 400 yards from their apartment. Rounding the last corner and peering over the construction for the new art center, she could see the two men on the fifth floor rocking in their chairs, smoke billowing from their illegal grill. Betty slowed down.

"Lord," she began again, "I'm going to ask forgiveness now . . . before I kill my husband!" She took a couple of deep breaths and walked into the lobby.

The elevator doors opened and Betty stepped in, pushing the fifth floor button and still trying to catch her breath. Once on her floor, she looked at Jack's front door, gave a disapproving head shake, then tried opening her door, but finding it locked. With Betty's memory slipping and with her habit of always misplacing her keys, Karl had hung a spare key behind the wreath that hung on their door. Betty had moved the spare key to the front of the wreath so she wouldn't forget where it was, something that drove Karl crazy. She made her way to their balcony, side by side with Jack's.

"How was the art lesson?" Karl saw her appear on their balcony.

"Did you two hear those loud explosions?" she asked.

Karl's expression changed, and he pointed down, "Our hillbillies were shooting clay targets from their balcony."

"Those crazy ladies. What made them stop?"

"Derrick," Jack answered.

"Speaking of Derrick, he's going to find out about your grill with all the smoke."

Still holding the cooking tongs, Karl pointed toward the grill with a smile. "His steak is on the grill."

A heavy knock sounded from Jack's front door, followed by the door opening and closing. "Speaking of the devil," Jack said, looking back in the apartment.

"Did you set those county bumpkins straight?" Karl asked.

Derrick shook his head, "They do have their part of crazy defined well. Hello Betty, how are you?"

"Have you bought her a ring yet?" Betty smiled, asking in a soft tone.

"You'll be the first to know." Derrick turned to Jack. "After tonight, the grill needs to go."

"Damn son, I just ordered fresh Maine lobster for tomorrow night, got you one too."

Derrick raised his left eyebrow. "Get rid of it after tomorrow night." He turned and leaned over the railing, giving Betty a kiss on the cheek. She had become a grandmother to him.

"Careful, that's my girl you're kissing," Karl smiled, giving Betty a butterfly feeling like she was back in high school with her sweetheart.

"Jack, keep my steak warm. I have to go check on Kat," Derrick added, heading out. Walking across the small court yard outside of the Tower apartments, he looked down a long pea gravel path leading to a fountain. He sighed at the sight of the fountain barely spewing water, then cut through part of the construction to the temporary art center.

Ducking under the caution tape that blocked part of the walkway, he was muttering to himself about the director taking a month off and leaving him in charge. "They say talking to yourself is the first stage of schizophrenia," an elderly gentlemen sitting on a park bench commented.

Derrick chuckled. "I'll take that into consideration Dr. Martin. You doing OK?"

"Yep, just waiting on the Mrs." The elderly doctor looked toward the sky. It had been a short month since his precious wife passed without him, and Derrick had taken a special interest in him and the Alzheimer's setting in. Derrick stopped his march toward the art center and sat on the bench beside the man. "Did I ever tell you how me and the Mrs. got caught in a rain storm in the middle of Bayou Tyche?"

"No, sir, tell me," Derrick lied, already having heard the story a few times.

The elderly man started in on the story as if it had just happened, and with hand motions, led into his favorite part, stealing a kiss. Derrick leaned back and settled in for the story, unaware of the spying eyes that watched through a healthy cluster of roses. Kat smiled with a warm feeling as she watched the man she loved give his attention to a recent widower. After giving them a few minutes, she walked around the roses and made her way toward the men.

Derrick cut his eyes in her direction, and without moving his head, watched as she approached, saying a prayer of thanks that he wasn't dreaming.

"I hope I'm not interrupting a deep conversation," she smiled.

"As a great philosopher said, 'Interruptions are merely a way to join good company.'"

Kat smiled, "Who said that?"

The old doctor smiled back, "I did." He pulled himself up from the bench, adding to Derrick, "You and I can finish my story later."

"You don't have to leave, we can—"

The man put his hand up. "Spend every moment with the one you love; it could be the last." He slowly walked down the paved path whistling a familiar song.

"So?" Kat paused, "Are you keeping the one you love waiting?"

Looking up at Kat, her hair starting to blend in with the evening sky, Derrick replied in a soft, warm tone, "You're right, I better go find her." He stood up and acted like he was walking past her.

She snatched his arm and swung his body into hers. "You better kiss me!" She leaned in with her lips meeting his. The whistling of the elderly man in the background and the cool breeze blowing through the roses made for a beautiful evening.

Chapter 3

Jack finished buttoning his shirt, then stood back and looked in the mirror mounted on the back of his closet door. "Yep, you still got it!" he said to himself, pointing a finger pistol at his reflection. Looking on the top shelf of his closet, he felt his way down the box of hats trying to choose the right one, landing on his favorite Italian straw fedora hat.

This evening was the traditional fall party that CBC had hosted ever since it opened its doors; it had a reputation of being a boring event, but with the new residents, the staff was questioning the outcome. Jack made his way to his balcony to catch the final act of the setting sun and sat in his chair clipping the end of a Cuban cigar.

"Are you not going to the fall party?" Karl asked, stepping out his balcony door.

"Yep," Jack answered.

"It starts in two minutes." Karl pointed at his Timex watch.

"And your point?"

"It'll take you thirty minutes to finish that cigar."

"You don't want to be the first person at the party."

He took a drag off the cigar, causing the end to form a glowing red head. "Fashionably late." He blew a puff of smoke in the air.

"See you there." Karl walked back in his apartment shaking his head in disapproval of Jack's style.

Jack rocked slowly back and forth, taking his time and enjoying his evening and smoke. Karl and Betty scurried out the door to the elevators, and before Karl could hit the down button the doors opened to the sight of the Stevens Sisters. "Good evening, Rutherfurds!" Violet yelled.

"It was," Karl groaned under his breath.

"June, you look beautiful!" Betty said looking at June's hippie-style dress, then at Violet, who was wearing shorts and a camouflage shirt. "And Violet . . . that's a nice shirt." She wasn't sure what to say.

"She's protesting the rule that she can't shoot targets from her balcony." June smiled and hugged Betty.

"It's against the law to shoot guns in the city limits," Karl added, determined to get in his two cents.

"That's what's wrong with our government, always trying to tell us what to do. Next thing you know, they'll outlaw the right to carry a gun in your purse," Violet replied.

"Well, actually . . . ," Karl started, but was quieted by Betty's elbow in his side.

"Where are you ladies heading?" Betty changed the subject.

"Jack told us to stop by before the party," June said, pushing the doorbell to Jack's apartment.

Betty stepped on the elevator, "We'll see you guys at the party." She motioned for Karl to follow her.

"Great! Just when the party is going to be good, Casanova is going to show up with the hippie and Charleton Heston's sister!" Karl grumbled as the elevator door closed.

Jack opened the door. "Come on in," he said, looking at Violet. "Going for the natural look this evening?"

"Those commies won't let me shoot my targets off the balcony." She pointed to her shirt, adding "Protesting!" Jack looked at her with a blank stare. "Surely that will make them change their minds." He looked at June, who was rolling her eyes.

"Come on, Goslin, let's smoke one of those fancy stogies before we hit this shin-dig."

Jack closed the door, "What's up with calling everyone by their last name?"

"Oh, its college football season, and she thinks she's a coach. Spends most of her Saturdays yelling at the TV," June said.

"Who do you root for?" he asked June.

With a big smile, she replied, "Oh, I root for the quarterback; they always have the cutest butts."

Jack started to refine his question, but thought it might be best to leave that conversation alone. He and June joined Violet on the balcony for a smoke and another glass of bourbon.

Down in the Huston Hall, just beyond the court yard and fitness center, Karl and Betty walked into the fall party, finding only a handful of people there, mostly staff. Karl helped Betty out of her sweater while holding her ice tea. "Where is everyone?" He glanced around the room, noticing the red and white checker table clothes, hay bales, wagon wheels, and a BBQ meal ready for serving.

"It's still early." Simon walked up, overhearing his question.

Karl looked at Simon, who was wearing a western shirt, jeans tucked in his boots, and a red bandana hanging out his back pocket. "What in the hell are you wearing?"

"All the staff wears western attire," Simon answered, tugging at his itchy shirt.

Speaking for only Betty to hear, Karl added, "I'd have to smoke reefer too to wear that."

"I'm sure he already has. Now be nice and let's visit with some people." Betty padded him on the chest and headed to a group of folks, leaving Karl to peel off towards the BBQ. Looking over the buffet with a plate balanced on his arm, Karl sampled a bite of food, then put it on his plate.

"You're going to be full before you get to the end of the line," Kat smiled.

"Gotta make sure it's not too spicy; Betty doesn't like spicy food."

"Bothers her stomach?"

"Bothers her nose."

"Nose?" Kat asked.

"Yep, spicy food upsets my stomach," he replied, studying the table for bread.

Kat widened her eyes, thinking that was more than she needed to know. "Well, let me know if you need anything." She looked past him and saw Betty talking with a new couple. "I see Betty has met the Carters."

Karl turned his head to see Betty talking to an African-American couple. "She doesn't know a stranger." They made eye contact, and Betty waved him over. "I'm eating!" he yelled back, only to receive a dirty look. He handed his plate to Kat. "Well, damn, hold this. I'll be right back."

"Honey, this is Terrell and Diana Carter. They just moved here," Betty introduced him.

"Nice to meet you," Karl shook Terrell's hand and started to walk back to his plate, but Betty stopped him. "Terrell is a retired pastor."

"Then he'll understand we need to get our food before the rush gets here."

"Now, honey, don't be rude," Betty insisted.

"No worries, I'm hungry too. I'll go with you," Reverend Carter answered.

"Damn good spread. They have BBQ chicken," Karl commented, walking back.

Rev. Carter cocked his head. "What are you implying? That we colored folks only eat chicken?"

Surprised and stuttering, Karl defended himself. "No.

I'm saying there's chicken on the table."

"I'm just messing with you," Rev. Carter laughed, elbowing Karl in the side and following him to the table.

Chapter 4

As predicted by Karl, Jack and the Stevens sisters rolled into the party three sheets in the wind and as giddy as teenagers. Violet's camouflage shirt created more attention than she had expected and with questions flying about her protest, the rest of the community agreed that they felt safer without target shooting from the balconies. But it wasn't Casanova, the hippie, or Charlton Hesston's sister who were the biggest interruption—it was the delivery of eight new golf carts. Kat squeezed through a group of residents. "Derrick."

She motioned for him to follow her.

"What's up?" He squeezed through the same group.

"There is a trailer of golf carts outside, and the driver is asking for you."

"Huh, they weren't supposed to be here until tomorrow. I'll take care of it." He tried to discreetly disappear outside but didn't notice the ten residents following close behind.

"There's my ride," a voice called from behind Derrick, and turning, he saw half the party walking outside with him.

"Folks, it will take a little while to unload them and then we will get them to their new owners," Derrick explained, trying to get everyone back to the party.

"Oh, it won't take no time," the driver replied, not understanding Derrick's plan.

Kat noticed Derrick's expression change and stepped beside him. "It's OK—this will just add some excitement to the party."

The driver handed Derrick a large envelope with titles and keys to the eight carts. Each golf cart was customized with its own flare, some with racing stripes, some with stereos, most with chrome wheels and two with spinning hubcaps, all extras professionally sold to the residents by a crafty and swindling salesman. All but one cart that was plain white with steel hubcaps and two seats—Karl's!

Everyone watched as the driver and his assistant unloaded each cart. "Ha, will you look at that! The wheels look like they are spinning," June shouted, pointing at a cart with spinning hubcaps.

Karl leaned over to Betty, asking "Who in the world would want a ghetto golf cart?"

"Just a BBQ chicken eatin' black pastor from the ghetto," Rev. Carter replied, overhearing Karl's statement.

Karl turned red with embarrassment. "A ghetto pastor?" Jack replied, standing behind them. "Where from?"

Rev. Carter turned to Jack. "Harlem." "Manhattan." Jack pointed to himself.

"A fellow New Yorker!" Rev. Carter shook his hand.

"I'm going to get more BBQ," Karl commented, rolling his eyes at the two New Yorkers greeting each other.

"Hey, Rutherfurd, tell me that's not your plain-jane cart," Violet yelled above the crowd.

"And what's wrong with plain?" he answered. "You're probably not going to live much longer! You need to spend some of that money you have stashed up there," Violet replied while eating a BBQ drumstick.

"Up where?" Karl asked.

"Don't ask that question in front of everyone," Jack stepped in to Karl's defense.

Karl thought for a minute. "You people are idiots," he concluded, storming back inside.

"One of these yours?" Jack asked Violet. "Nope, I haven't decided what I want yet."

Kat spoke up and asked everyone to head back inside for a few announcements, and then they would give the paperwork and keys to the new owners of the carts.

"I see you have met Karl," Jack said to Rev. Carter.

"Yep, he got embarrassed thinking I was offended about being stereotyped over a chicken comment." "That sounds like him. Good guy, though." Jack put his hand on Rev. Carter's back. "Come on back inside;

we have some great watermelon too." Rev. Carter started laughing and followed his new friend back in the party.

Once back inside, a line quickly formed in front of Derrick for paperwork and keys for the new owners of their carts. Kat laughed at the persistence and encouraged Derrick to just go with it. "Maybe we can have a race around the campus and see whose cart is the fastest," she suggested, trying to lighten the fact that his party was crashed by golf carts.

"That's all I need: eight wrecked golf carts along with eight new patients in the health center of CBC," Derrick grumbled, handing the last set of keys out.

Kat placed her arm around his waist and laid her head on his shoulders trying to comfort him. An elderly lady walked by with a walker. "Get a room," she grumbled.

Derrick gave Kat a look that said he couldn't win for losing tonight, but she just batted her eyes back at him. "You want to get a room?" she teased him, then pinched his butt.

"Stop that," he jumped forward, turning red. "I better go check on Jack."

"I'm sure Jack is fine. I'll see you after the party, supper?" She smiled, getting a smile and head nod back. Derrick found the Stevens sisters talking with Diana

Carter. "Where is Jack?"

Violet pointed to him standing in the corner hovering over a plate of BBQ and solving all the world's problems with Rev. Carter. Heading towards them, Derrick noticed Karl standing at the window, peering at something outside. "Everything OK?" he asked.

"Making sure those dumbasses don't scratch my golf cart."

"I'm sure they know what they're doing," Derrick assured him.

Before Karl could answer, both Rev. Carter and Jack walked up. "Derrick, Rev. Carter tells me you are taking them on their orientation trip in a few days."

"We have a couple of other new residents coming that want to make the trip too," Derrick answered.

"If you have room and need help, I'd love to volunteer my services," Jack said.

Derrick shook his head, thinking that if he could leave Simon behind to help on campus, he would not be so overwhelmed when he got back. "Let me think about that." He looked at Rev. Carter. "Rev, are you finding everything here OK?"

"I am, thank you. And please call me Ty-rail." "I thought your name was Terrell?" Karl asked. "Ty-rail."

"How do you spell that?" Karl asked. "T.E.R.R.E.L.L."

"Terrell!" Karl answered.

"We pronounce it Ty-rail," the reverend insisted.

Karl looked on perplexed, thinking about how he could get out of the stereotyping predicament he kept getting himself into.

"I'm just messing with you," Rev. Carter slapped him on his back.

Chapter 5

After a long and interesting night, Derrick poured himself another cup of coffee from the small kitchenette in the administration building connected to the welcome center. Then, balanced his cup, file folders, and construction report while walking to the conference room. A half-dozen people, joined by the construction crew foreman and Katlyn Rose, and new additions to the group, were already in their chairs for the meeting.

"Good morning, everyone." Derrick set his coffee cup down and dropped his file folder. "Everyone knows John, our neighborly construction foreman. And if you haven't met her yet, this is Kat." Everyone chuckled; Kat was no new face to CBC. "I'm not sure how the director juggled not only her time, but the endless files that come with this job," he added out loud.

"She had other people do it." A young lady smiled, meaning no disrespect.

Derrick smiled back. "Yep, me. And actually the director asked Kat to step in while she is gone this month to help me." He fell into his chair. "All right, let's get down to business."

Everyone looked down at the agenda printed out for them, to the first line, reading Fitness Instructor. "Why is fitness instructor written?" another lady asked.

Derrick looked at Deanna, the instructor, and gave her a nod. "Well," she started, "I have loved my time here at CBC, but my husband is being relocated with his job. So this will be my last week."

An emotional sigh fell over the room. "Deanna, you are so good with our residents," someone in the room commented. "You will be greatly missed. Where are you moving?"

"My husband is an architect with a resort company, and we have been asked to move to Hawaii."

"Oh, bless your suffering heart," the same lady added, followed by a laugh in the room.

"Rough life." Derrick shook his head, "But Deanna is departing on great terms, having replaced herself with a well-educated colleague. She graduated with a girl named Jaqueline Silva, and the director met with her before she left and hired her on the spot." Derrick passed out a picture and bio of the new hire.

"We better check the batteries in our defibrillators!" one of the ladies added, looking at Jaqueline's picture.

Another person at the table added, "Is she American?

She's so dark complexioned and beautiful."

"She is Brazilian," Deanna added.

While the others were complimenting the picture, Kat leaned over to Derrick. "And you met with her?" she asked.

Clueless, he smiled. "I did."

"Why didn't you tell me that Deanna was leaving?" "I don't know. I just didn't think about it." He looked around the table, "OK, folks, Jaqueline will be joining us tomorrow, so please make her feel welcome." He paused, "Oh yea, she told me that she likes to be called Jaqs."

Kat lifted one of her eyebrows at Derrick and mumbled under her breath, "Oh, really."

"Now to the construction," Derrick said, still clueless about Kat's comments and questions. "Can you give us an update on the bridge, art center, and new restaurant?"

The foreman sat up straighter in his chair. "The bridge is finished, and we are just doing some touch ups with the lights."

"The walkway seems tight with just one lane for carts to cross," someone interrupted.

"That is what we had to build with both the budget and codes. I suggest putting up a 'Slow' sign on both ends of the bridge and asking residents to respect those walking over the bridge. The parking on the beach side will fit fourteen carts," the foreman added.

Derrick handed out another piece of paper, "Everyone who has a golf cart will need to attend a driver's class and abide by the rules on where you can drive your cart."

"And the sooner the better," a lady pointed out the window. Everyone turned in their chairs to see Karl driving his cart through the courtyard and roses while yelling at people to get out of the way.

Derrick took a deep breath; he had expressed his opinion to the director about allowing carts, but was greatly outvoted, "Will someone please get Karl off the paths before someone gets hurt!"

"I'll go," Kat said, laughing.

The foreman gently grabbed Kat's arm as she tried to leave. "Before you go, you will be glad to hear that we are ahead of schedule for the art center, and it will open next week," he said with a flirtatious smile.

"Best news of the day," she smiled and walked out. "The restaurant?" Derrick asked with a smirk.

"It is also ahead of schedule and will be ready to open in two weeks."

"So all construction will be done?" someone asked.

"The big construction will be, but myself and a few others will be here for an additional two weeks tying up loose ends and finishing the landscape." He closed his folder.

Kat jogged after Karl, who was determined to clear the pathway with his cart. "Karl!" Kat yelled, trying to catch him.

Turning his cart too sharp and hanging his back wheel on the curb allowed Kat enough time to catch him, "Damn cart path isn't wide enough!" Karl yelled as she caught him.

"Karl, the carts have to stay on the designated areas."

"We bought the damn things so we don't have to walk!"

"Designated areas only." She gave him a stern look. "Scoot over and I'll drive you out of here."

Without an argument, Karl slid over and gave Kat the wheel. "Where is Betty?" she asked.

"She won't ride with me."

"I wonder why?" Kat giggled as she slowly drove out of the courtyard and onto a paved path that was designated for the carts.

An elderly man yelled at her to get the cart out of the courtyard before she could reach the paved path. "We know! We know!" Karl yelled back at him.

"It's OK," she tried to calm him down, then saw Jack walking out of the Loft apartments. "What is he doing?" "I don't know! Haven't seen him all morning," Karl said.

"Keeping up with your neighbor?" she smiled. "No!" Karl covered. "We just normally have coffee on our balconies. Which I might add are too damn close." Jack gave them a casual wave, carrying his white sport coat over his shoulder and whistling a happy tune as he headed back to his apartment.

Chapter 6

Rev. Carter and Dianna walked through the store picking out snacks and drinks for their stroll to the beach. After spending $23.45 for two bottles of water, a small package of chips, and sixteen sticks of beef jerky, the two walked out, bumping into the Stevens sisters. June, dressed in her normal flowery muumuu dress, and Violet, wearing a large thick cover-up, stopped in front of the Carters.

"Hello, ladies," Rev. Carter smiled, gripping his stash of beef jerky in one hand.

Violet cocked her head at the amount of beef jerky. "Expecting Jesus to come back today?" she asked.

"Excuse me?"

"A handful of jerky isn't going to get you through the apocalypse," Violet replied.

Rev. Carter looked at his hand. "No, but it will get me through a sunset," he smiled.

"Not much of a romantic, is he? With all that jerky breath at sunset," Violet said to Dianna, who was speechless. "But know this, when the apocalypse comes, I've got 83 cases of MREs and 6,000 rounds of ammo. Doubt seriously God's gonna take me on round one."

The Carters looked at each other. "Round one?" Rev asked her.

"You know, when the Jesus people go up in the clouds. I figure God is gonna leave a few people down here to wipe out the zombies and the other sons of bitches that don't make the cut," Violet added.

June stepped in to save the Carters. "We haven't officially met. I'm June, and this is my sister Violet." She reached out a hand to shake.

Dianna smiled, "We are the Carters." She shook June's hand.

"We are heading to the beach and can walk with you," June said.

"Oh, boy," Rev Carter said with a smirk.

"Are you going to watch the sunset?" Dianna asked, feeling a civil conversation coming with June.

"No, Violet likes to swim this time of day." Dianna turned to Violet. "Isn't it cold?"

"Sweetheart, at this age and weight, the only thing I feel is the kick of my twelve gauge shotgun and a good bowel movement!"

Dianna's eyes grew twice their size as she looked back at June. "Me, on the other hand, I am going to my Mother Earth Yoga Dance class just down the beach."

"I know I'm probably going to regret this, but what is Mother Earth dance class?" Rev. Carter was hesitant to ask.

"It's her mumbo jumbo paying respect to earth's creator and other bullshit," Violet put her hand on his shoulder. "Sorry for the French." She smiled.

Rev. Carter laughed. "Quite OK, I'm not sure what to say. I do believe God created the earth, though."

June waved toward him nonchalantly. "Of course she did." She paused, "With the help of a few other men."

Dianna turned to her husband with a death stare not to reply just as Karl and Betty pulled up in their golf cart. The four stopped at the foot of the bridge with Karl blocking their way, Violet slowly peered around June and locked eyes with Karl.

"Violet." He stared back.

Rutherfurd." She replied, not giving the Carters an easy feeling about their meeting.

"I see you've met the Stevens sisters," Karl said to Rev.

Carter.

"Yes, we were just talking about Mother Earth helping God create the earth. I think." He looked at June.

Betty interrupted them. "June, I love that dress. You going to your class?"

"I am," June answered.

"We're going to the beach, bye!" Karl blurted, slamming down the gas pedal and causing Betty's head to bobble back and forth and spilling half her ice tea, but never losing the smile that was on her face. "They're out to get me!" Karl yelled, topping the bridge.

"Who?" Betty said, trying to balance what was left in her glass.

"The hippie, the gun toting communist, and now the black preacher!"

Betty, patting him on the leg, replied, "Now, now dear. Not everyone is out to get you."

Their golf cart came to a rest in one of the parking spots that paralleled the beach, and Karl climbed out to help Betty so she wouldn't have to set down her ice tea. Grabbing a couple of chairs from the back of the cart, they walked slowly through the deep sand that had been raked the previous day. A gentle breeze coming from the gulf welcomed them to a soon-to-be spectacular show of the sky's fireworks and colors. Karl carried the chairs, helping his love for over a half century find the perfect place to watch the sunset. "It's a beach, all the spots are good," he insisted.

She smiled without a comment and pointed to a place that kids had recently built a sand castle. They unfolded their chairs and settled in for the show after Karl kicked over the castle. His arm rest just touched Betty's chair, and after shifting his weight to settle his chair in the sand, he turned up his palm, inviting Betty's frail hand to lock fingers with his.

The Carters split ways with June and Violet and found a spot on the sand close to the water to watch the sun take its final bow of the evening. June stayed with

Violet to watch the explosions of red and orange that cast indescribable reflections on a calm gulf. Karl turned and glanced back at his balcony and could see a puff of white smoke come from Jack's balcony.

The residents of CBC certainly gave each other a hard time, but understood the importance of embracing a brilliant show that only happened once a day.

After the sun was gone, June said goodbye to Violet and made her way to her class down the beach. Karl and Betty made it back to their cart as the Carters stepped onto the pavement of the parking lot. "Beautiful sunset," Dianna observed.

"Oh, it's something that never changes and always worth the watch," Betty smiled.

"Karl, I wouldn't have taken you as a sunset type of guy," Rev. Carter said.

Karl turned to the gulf just in time to see Violet shed her cover up and reveal her two-piece bikini, "The sunset temporally blinds me so I won't have to watch that." He pointed to Violet.

Rev. Carter stood speechless with his mouth open. "What is that around her neck?" Dianna asked.

"She replaced her bikini straps with bungee cords." Betty answered, then whispered, "She says it helps hold her girls up." She smiled at Dianna. Rev. Carter never moved, hypnotized by the lack of clothing.

Chapter 7

Jack sat at his computer screen clicking away with his mouse, "Nope, Nope." He repeated over and over, looking at something on the monitor. He backed away rubbing his eyes, then glancing back at the clock reading 12:15 a.m., he shook his head and gave up on his research. Walking out onto his balcony to take in a deep breath of salt air, he saw Karl leaning on his railing. "Evening," he greeted him.

"What are you doing still up?" Karl asked.

"Oh, looking at something on the computer." Jack joined him.

Karl studied him for a second. "What were you doing coming out of the Loft apartments yesterday morning?"

Jack twitched his eyebrows. "Entertaining Sylvia Westheimer."

Karl shook his head. "I'm sorry I asked." "What are you doing up?" Jack asked.

"The older I get, the less sleep I get."

Jack noticed Derrick and Kat walking over the bridge coming from the beach. "Love seems the swiftest, but it is the slowest of all growths. No man or woman really knows what perfect love is until they have been married a quarter of a century," Jack quoted.

Karl looked at him as if he were drunk and asked, "What the hell has got you quoting Mark Twain at midnight?" Jack pointed to the couple. "And what in the hell do you know about being married twenty-five years?"

Jack looked at him. "Something I'll never know." He slipped back into his apartment.

Karl yelled, "I didn't mean it like that." Jack stuck his hand out the door before it closed and gave him a thumbs up, insinuating all was well. Karl hadn't known Jack very long, but knew something was amiss with him.

Below, Derrick and Kat held hands as they patrolled the courtyard, coming upon the fountain that had given Derrick a headache for the last two months. "You had it fixed." Kat observed, seeing the water spray out of the fountain in a uniform manner.

"No," Derrick smirked.

Small clouds quickly floated by a full moon with a steady southern wind generating a small gust through the campus. Derrick and Kat sat on a bench that was one of the more popular spots in the courtyard. "Why didn't you tell me about hiring the new fitness instructor?" Kat asked. "I don't know, I really didn't think about it," he answered. "Why?"

"Well, according to her picture, she is absolutely gorgeous."

He smiled, "We'll have the healthiest group of elderly men this side of the Mississippi." Then he started to sense her hesitation about his decision. "Don't worry, there's only one girl in this place I'm interested in," he added.

"Violet?" Kat grinned.

"Well, with her new bungee cord bikini, you never know." He laughed.

"Speaking of Violet." She pointed to the Stevens' light still on. "What in the world do you think they are doing?" Kat asked.

"We could go find out or go take a quick swim in the indoor pool?"

"I don't have a swimsuit—" She stopped in mid-sentence, "Oh." She smiled and stood up. And like a bunch of teenagers they quickly ran through the courtyard to the fitness center and its small heated indoor pool.

Reaching the door, they were greeted by one of the residents. "Good evening, Mr. St. Clair," the man said loudly.

"Mr. Johnson?" Derrick greeted him back, confused as to what he was doing at the door. "What are you doing out, and why are you guarding the door?"

He answered in a loud voice with his head slightly turned toward the door, "Why, Mr. St. Clair, I'm not guarding the door."

"If you don't mind." Derrick gently pushed by him and opened the door to a group of people in bathing suits with wine glasses scattered throughout the pool. Everyone froze at Derrick's presence, and rightfully so, since CBC had a strong policy about the pool closing at 10 p.m. and no alcohol being allowed. Violet gave Kat a small grin and wave as she entered behind Derrick.

"OK, folks, you know the rules about alcohol around the pool and no swimming after 10 p.m.!" he said, everyone still frozen in place like a bunch of middle school kids who had just been caught.

Kat took Derrick's hand and pulled him back to the door. "Thirty more minutes and the party needs to end," she said.

"Kat we have—" She put her finger to his lips. "You're starting to sound more like the director."

She lowered her voice, adding, "Let them have fun, plus how bad can it be? They kept Violet clothed."

The door shut behind Derrick and Kat. "Johnson!" Violet started, "You said you'd alert us if anyone showed up."

"That was a dumb idea; you people couldn't hear an atomic bomb detonating outside the door," Mr. Johnson replied.

"Kat, I worry about . . ." She placed her finger on Derrick's lips again.

"Don't. They are fine." She replaced her finger with her lips to distract him, which worked.

Chapter 8

The following morning, Derrick walked out of his office to refill his coffee cup with the new coffee from Nicaragua that a resident had suggested. After small talk with the director's receptionist he returned to his cell phone buzzing with a text, and after searching under the clutter on his desk, he saw a message from Kat asking about lunch. He leaned against his desk responding that he wasn't sure if he could because today was going to be Jaqueline's first day and he might be busy showing her around.

"Excuse me!" Kat stared at the message, then replied, but before Derrick had time to see the return message, a light knock came from his open door, and looking up, he was greeted by a tall, dark-complexioned woman.

"Mr. St. Clair?" she asked with an accent.

"Call me Derrick; you must be Jaqueline." He reached out to greet her. Using only her finger tips, she returned the handshake. "Please have a seat." He pointed to one of the chairs facing his desk.

"Please, call me Jaqs." She flattened out her dress and sat with her legs facing to the side, the light blue dress only causing the complexion of her legs to appear darker, and with a low-cut blouse, her cleavage was just as exposed as her legs. Derrick's first thought was that it was not the best dress to wear on your first day, but since she was the fitness instructor, he brushed off the thought. After finding her resume on his desk, Derrick commented, pointing at the resume, that "You have worked with a retirement community before."

"Yes, two. One in Miami and another in my home country of Brazil.

After studying her degree and qualifications, Derrick added, "Well, I'm not sure if we are as fancy as the property in Miami, but our residents are great people."

"I am sure they are."

"Would you like a tour?" Derrick asked.

"I would love that." They walked out together, leaving her handbag in the chair and his cell phone on the desk. After greeting everyone in the office, they walked outside and started in the courtyard, where a dozen or so folks were enjoying the day. As if shot with a stun gun, all the men froze in their tracks, unable to move. One lady popped her husband on the back of the head to snap him out of his trance over Jaqs following Derrick. As they exited the courtyard, one man turned to another, "Who is that?"

"Maybe we crossed over and that was St. Peter and one of his angels."

"St. Peter sure looks a lot like Derrick."

Since Derrick had not answered his text from Kat, she walked to the office, noticing the men in a more chipper mood than normal, but didn't ask and continued her trek to the office. Walking past the receptionist, she walked into Derrick's office to find his cell phone on the desk and a handbag in the chair. She snatched it up and walked into the hall. "Whose handbag?" she asked the receptionist.

"That probably belongs to Jaqs," she smiled. "Have you seen her? She is gorgeous."

"Huh!" Kat threw the handbag back in the office and headed out to find him.

Derrick and Jaqs were just passing the bridge when a group of residents stormed up from the beach, all talking at the same time. "They moved our chairs" was the only thing Derrick could understand.

"OK, everyone simmer down. Who moved what?" he asked.

By now, the men in the group had noticed Jaqs and had become just as mute as the men in the courtyard, so one of the ladies spoke up. "The lifeguard from the resort next door said his manager asked him to move all our things."

Derrick could see they were upset. "OK, I'll have a word with them." He started up the bridge and noticed no-one was following him. Instead they surrounded Jaqs like a bunch of groupies at a rock-n-roll concert. "Can you give me a second?" he asked Jaqs.

"Yes," she smiled, answering the questions that the women were throwing at her while the men stood there in their vegetable-state comas.

Topping the bridge, he saw Karl on the beach with his finger in a young lifeguard's face. "Great," Derrick said to himself, and getting closer, he heard Karl giving him a piece of his mind that would make a sailor blush.

"Karl!" Derrick put his hand on his shoulder. "I'll handle this."

"By God, I never thought I'd ask for Violet's help, but I have a good mind to get her and her 50 cal. she keeps talking about!"

The young lifeguard took another big swallow and looked at Derrick, "You can't be moving the belongings of our residents." Derrick said.

"I am just following orders from my manager," the boy said.

Derrick noticed a well-dressed man step onto the beach from the resort. "Is that him?"

"Yes sir."

The man approached, asking "Do we have a problem, gentlemen?"

"You damn right we have a problem!" Karl stepped back into the conversation.

Derrick waved him down. "I'll take care of it." He turned back to the manager, adding, "Seems we have a misunderstanding of the boundary. You see, our property line comes through here." He pointed down.

"Well, we have a rather large resort that requires more room. I believe you are mistaken and that we have a written agreement that allows us to take fifty feet of your property."

"I don't know of any written agreement, and we need all of our property now that we have a safer access to the beach."

"Yes, I know." he answered in a snotty tone. "Now I have to deal with my clients seeing half-dressed old people lounging in the sun."

Karl almost passed out. "Old people!" His voice shot up two octaves.

"I believe you are out of line, and I would suggest you stay to your side of the beach," Derrick replied, feeling a little of Karl's anger.

"I will have my attorneys contact you with the agreement." The snotty manager turned his back, snapped his finger for the lifeguard to follow, and walked back to his resort.

"You tell your attorneys to shove that   "

Derrick interrupted Karl. "Don't get worked up over them. I can handle them."

Karl was still craning over Derrick's head, looking at the manager walking away, "So can I!"

Chapter 9

Derrick walked back across the bridge to find a larger crowd of people had gathered around Jaqs with tons of questions, mostly men. Two of the original crowd met him at the foot of the bridge awaiting an answer from him, and after a few minutes of convincing them that everything was OK, they returned to the questions to Jaqs. Derrick squeezed his way through the crowd of groupies. "OK, folks, Jaqs will be starting her fitness classes tomorrow, so you can ask her questions then," Derrick said, trying to peel her away.

But it wasn't Derrick that broke up the crowd; instead, a golf cart driving through the middle of them with the driver yelling at them to get the hell out of the way divided the group. Derrick shook his head as Karl aimed toward his parking spot, a spot where he had previous spray painted his name on the curb—another issue for Derrick.

"Shall we?" Derrick pointed toward the fitness center and store.

Jaqs looked around to make sure it was clear. "I think so. This is the first retirement community I can think of that allows the residents to have their own carts."

"That might not last," Derrick said, walking.

"Is that a fire?" She pointed toward the balconies of the Tower apartments.

Derrick looked up to see Jack sitting in his rocking chair holding a spatula while the smoke poured out of his grill. "No, but we need to stop by." His expression changed.

Half way to the fitness center, the two of them were greeted by Kat, who did her best to hide her true thoughts of Derrick hiring Jaqs. "Hey," Derrick replied to the 5'6" girl waiting on them in the middle of the path.

"Hello," she replied with a hint of sarcasm. "Jaqs, this is Kat," Derrick introduced them.

Jaqs went to shake her hand and saw the remnants of leftover paint in the creases of her knuckles. "Oh, honey, is this paint on your hands?"

"Hence, the art instructor," she replied.

"I can help with getting that paint removed." She moved in to whisper, "Dirty hands will only run off men." She smiled, unaware of her competitive presence.

Kat pulled her hand back. "My hands are just fine— it's part of my trade."

"Come find me if you need help," Jaqs smiled, still unaware.

Kat looked at Derrick. "Can we talk?" She motioned to a bench off to the side and in privacy.

"Can it wait? We have to go talk to Jack about his grill."

"We?" She slightly turned her head and lifted her eyebrows at him.

"Derrick, show me the fitness center," Jaqs requested, then looked at Kat. "I'm sure you don't mind waiting, I am excited to see where I will be teaching." Then she looked back at Derrick, adding, "You will be attending my class?"

Derrick laughed. "I don't know."

Kat, who was still in the same pose, asked, "You don't know?"

"And, honey, you could use some toning too; I expect to see you in my class tomorrow." She walked on without Derrick.

Kat stood speechless, staring daggers through Derrick. "Sorry, I'll catch up with you in a few," Derrick replied, then caught back up with Jaqs.

Fuming with flames starting to show, Kat stood thinking that he couldn't be this clueless, and after a few deep breaths, she looked up at the fifth floor and saw Jack sitting in his chair. She wasn't much of a drinker, but instead of exploding in the pathway, she marched toward the lobby and elevators of the Tower Apartments.

Jack opened his front door to the knocking. "I thought a gorilla was knocking," he replied to Kat, whose knuckles were red from knocking.

"I need a drink." She pushed through the door. "Come on in," he replied, closing the door and wondering what was going on and why everyone thought his place was the local bar. He turned to find Kat pouring a glass of bourbon. "Go easy on that."

"I need something to put these flames out!" She tossed back a shot.

"That bourbon isn't the answer—it's strong enough to add flames. Can I interest you in a glass of water?"

She poured another shot. "If he just thinks he can parade around here with that Brazilian goddess by his side, he has another think coming!" She threw back another shot.

"Jaqs." Jack replied, walking back to his chair. "You've meet her?"

"Not yet."

"How do you know . . . ?"

He interrupted her, "Single radar." He pointed to his head.

"I don't need jokes right now."

"Relax. It's his job to see that all us crazy old folks are taken care of. With her qualifications, she can help most people around here."

"How do you know that?"

"Derrick talked to me," he answered.

"Oh, he talks to you, but leaves me in the dark."

"I can understand that you might be upset at him hiring her, she's tall, dark complexioned, with paralyzing brown eyes."

"Jack!" She brought him out of his daydream. "Sorry, but you don't have anything to worry about.

That boy loves you. He is going to be around people, and you can't fly off the handle at him every time a beautiful woman shows up."

"But he didn't tell me that "

"And that should show you. If he felt like he owed you an explanation of hiring someone beautiful, then you should worry."

She sat back in her chair in thought. "He does love me, doesn't he?"

"Talks about you constantly." He stood up to check the steaks on the grill.

"What does he say?"

Jack looked over the railing at Derrick and Jaqs as they walked to the Tower Apartments with a small gaggle of men following. "We're going to see who has a bad heart around here in the next few days," he said to himself.

"What?" She didn't hear him.

"He talks about your future. Now, no more questions.

I can't betray the bro code on talking to each other." She laughed, "The bro code?"

"You know, the code that states that whatever guys talk about stays with the guys." Jack smiled. Then another knock came from his door. "Huh, normally Karl doesn't knock." He walked to the door and opened it to find Derrick and Jaqs.

"Jack, you know I said you have to get rid of the grill."

Jack shook his head and waved his hand across his neck, hinting to keep his voice down. "OK, I'll get rid of it tomorrow. Thanks for coming." He tried to shut the door.

"What are you doing?" Derrick put his hand on the door, "Is Mrs. Westheimer here?" He craned over Jack, looking into the apartment.

"Hum, yea. Come back later." Jack tried to get rid of them.

"Hello again, Kat," Jaqs said, seeing Kat walk into Jack's kitchen.

Jack's head fell. "Come on in," he replied.

"Mrs. Westheimer isn't here. What are you doing?" Derrick asked Kat.

"Are those filets on your grill?" Jaqs took a deep breath and walked toward the balcony.

Jack looked at the body of Jaqs as she walked past, then back to Derrick and Kat. "You kids play nice." He hustled to his balcony. "Why, yes, I had them flown in just yesterday. Would you like to try a piece?"

Kat watched Jack disappear onto his balcony. "Things will never change."

"Are you mad at me?" Derrick asked. "Yes, and no."

"Well what is it? And what did I do?" he asked, and then it hit him. "Jaqs?"

"I haven't seen you this interested in showing someone—"

"You haven't seen me as a director, either," he interrupted her. "It's my job, and remember, I didn't hire her. Relax, you're my girl and only you!"

"I'm your girl?" She grinned and wrapped her arms around him, pulling herself in tight, unaware of the eyes from the balcony watching her.

I've never not gotten the man I wanted, Jaqs grinned.

Chapter 10

Violet dug through the cabinets in their kitchen searching for a large plastic spoon. "I know we packed it. Shouldn't it be with your wine making supplies?" June yelled while filing her nails at the table. Violet looked up from the cabinet in thought and then headed to the pantry to search in a plastic bin. Violet had started her wine making back in Arkansas when she overheard a few women speaking about buying Muscatine wine from a local. The thought of making and selling wine intrigued her, but the thought of eluding the law interested her even more.

Violet had tried many different recipes for her Muscatine wine, but came up with bitter juice and a repair bill when she blew up the back corner of their porch. So she gave up and ordered grapes from a vineyard in California, and after two tries came up with a tasteful and delightful wine. It wasn't long before she had a group of ladies from the local Baptist church buying her wine and passing the word.

That is, until one day a knock came from the front door and Violet found the preacher threating to turn her in if she continued to sell alcohol to his congregation. But after convincing him with new pews for the church building and new hymnals, he allowed her to sell to the ladies. And every Sunday morning from the pulpit, he would roll his eyes at the half dozen hungover widows.

"Why don't you use a wooden spoon?" June asked. "Sterilization is key to making wine, and plastic is better. Ha! Found it!" She emerged from the pantry. Unscrewing the large top off her 6 gallon carboy, she began stirring the red grape juice.

"You look like a witch stirring her brew," June giggled. "If I were a witch, you'd be a toad. And I'm not stirring— I'm degassing the wine," she replied.

"That's not the only thing around here that needs degassing," June said under her breath.

After stirring the six gallons of wine, Violet screwed the top back on and wheeled the carboy to the spare bedroom that she had turned into her cellar. She placed the carboy against the wall with the others next to a rack with 25 other 6-gallon containers of wine. She grinned with pride at her 750 gallons of wine, enough to supply most of the restaurants in southern Alabama.

"I'm going to have to get Simon to come help me take down some wine off the top rack this afternoon," she said.

"He's such a nice boy," June replied, still filing her nails.

"He's too young for you," Violet answered, followed by a giggle from June.

"Let's just hope the law doesn't come knocking," June replied, pointing her finger nail file at the thirty plus guns Violet had hanging on the wall in their living room and kitchen.

"Why? It's legal to have guns!"

"If you start growing tobacco, you'd be a one-stop shop for the ATF."

Violet rubbed her chin. "I wonder how close the nearest tobacco farm is?"

June glanced up at the clock. "Oh dear, I'm going to be late." She dropped her file, grabbed a yoga mat, and headed to the door.

"Where are you going? Isn't it early for your reefer class?"

"I'm going to Jaqs' new class here in the fitness center," she yelled from the hallway before the door could shut.

Once in the lobby of the Tower Apartments, June could see a large group of people forming at the fitness center; ironically, it was mostly men. She pushed her way through some of the men, who clearly had no clue about fitness, and ran into Jack. "What's with all the commotion?" she asked him.

"A hot Brazilian moves in to CBC, and you have to ask that question?" Jack smiled.

June scanned the area. "Well, if she has this kind of impact, we will be the fittest retirement community around."

"Are you kidding me? The first time she bends over to stretch, ninety percent of these men are going to stroke out!"

"She is beautiful; I wonder if she has any Brazilian beauty secrets?"

"I don't know about secrets, but if you don't own stock in Viagra, now's the time to buy," Jack replied as the doors opened.

Just as a rock star would take the stage at a concert, the crowd at CBC broke into applause when Jaqs walked in the doorway. "Oh my, this is a few more than I expected," she exclaimed, and after looking at the crowd, added, "Everyone grab a mat from inside and let's set up over on the grassy area near the fountain."

"I'll save you a spot," June told Jack, following Jaqs to the grassy area. After an intensive instruction session on how to form five lines, Jaqs began her class by having the residents sit on their mat with their legs crossed—a feat that knocked out half the men in group with their non-agile flexibility.

Jack, who had taken two mats to protect his white slacks, sat with his legs crossed. "I think I'm stuck," he commented to June, who giggled and told him to hush.

Jaqs joined her hands together in a praying form and asked the group to remain silent and breathe in through their nostrils and out their mouths, and for five minutes the crowd tried their best to follow her instructions.

"What in the hell is going on down there!" Karl bellowed out from his balcony.

"Oh, that's Jaqs new class. I bet I have time to join," Betty replied.

"Looks like a Muslim group praying." He looked closer and saw Jack among the group, "That sell-out! He's just there because of the Brazilian girl." He looked closer, "And why in the hell is the preacher there?" He spotted Rev. Carter a few rows from Jack.

Karl turned to see why Betty wasn't answering him just in time to see the front door close. In frustration, he dragged his chair to the rail and continued to watch the group as they followed the instructions of their limber instructor. With every pose, two to three people would either fall over to the side, face down, or land on their back.

"Huh! This might be more entertaining than I thought," Karl said, thinking about popping a bag of popcorn.

Chapter 11

During lunch, the two main topics were the new class that Jaqs was teaching in the mornings and Jaqs. Like a high school cafeteria, the women were on one side discussing the class and outfits to buy, and on the other were the widowers talking about Jaqs and her outfits. A new record was set at CBC for the number of nitro pills consumed during lunch. Kat finished loading her tray with a ham rollup and a fresh garden salad, already tired of smiling at residents asking who were asking if she had met Jaqs while she was searching the café for Derrick. Spotting him sitting with his normal crew, Jack, Karl, and the new reverend, Kat made her way to them.

"Is this seat taken?" Jaqs asked Derrick, pointing beside him. Before he could explain that it was saved for Kat, all the men at the table blurted in unison, "No, sir!" Kat didn't notice until she reached the table that her seat was now taken, and not happy it, she set her tray next to Jack, who put his arm around her. Saying "This is working out perfect," he tried to lighten the tension that was building.

"Yeah, just perfect," she said, looking at Derrick, who was trying to explain through expressions that Jaqs had invited herself to sit down. It wasn't helping matters that all the attention at the table was drawn to Jaqs, whose low-cut blouse caused a few to miss their mouths with the food.

"Where is Diana?" Kat asked Rev. Carter.

"What's that?" he replied, snapping out of his trance and turning his attention to the end of the table.

"Diana, is she around?"

"Oh, yes. She is at the store. I believe we are signing up for your intro to painting class. Are there still openings?" he asked.

With a smirk, Kat answered, "Yes, seems more people are interested in fitness right now."

"Wait! It's not the same time?" he asked.

With an eyebrow raised, she replied a curt "No" and glanced down at Derrick, who was fixated on his phone, reading a message.

He looked up and caught the stare from Kat. "Seems our neighbors are marking off the beach. I need to walk over; do you want to go?" he asked Kat. With the tension well known through the community, everyone at the table simultaneously answered "Yes" at the same time. Derrick looked at everyone. "I was thinking that just Kat and I walk over, so you guys stay here and enjoy lunch." He grabbed his tray and followed Kat to the door.

Holding it open, he added to Kat, "I'm sorry—I was saving you a seat and Jaqs just sat down."

"You could have told her you were saving it?" "I don't want to be rude."

She cut her eyes at him, then noticed the trail of golf carts slowly following them. The first cart was Karl and Jack, followed by Rev. Carter, then four other carts. She giggled under her breath and waited for Derrick to notice. Once they walked past the parking lot and stepped onto the beach, all six golf carts raced for parking, causing Derrick to notice. "Good grief," he muttered.

"Kinda reminds me of a motorcycle gang," Kat laughed.

"Geriatrics on wheels!" Jack replied, overhearing her. Derrick looked back at nine residents following him onto the beach. "Don't worry, we've got your back," Karl said with a snarl.

"Please stay here while I talk to their manager," Derrick pleaded with them, then turned and walked to the manager of the resort, who was ordering his beach attendants to set out chairs and umbrellas.

"I see you brought back up," The manager laughed, pointing behind Derrick at the nine people that were on his heels.

"Our boundaries are clearly marked, and I have checked into this so-called agreement—it doesn't exist. I am trying to be nice, so please keep your chairs and umbrellas on your side of the beach," Derrick replied.

"Don't be nice!" Karl barked standing behind them. Derrick waved at him, trying to keep him and the dirty "half dozen" quiet.

"Listen!" the manager started. "We have been using this area for years, but now you build a bridge so that your old people don't get hit by a car—"

"Old people?" Karl's voice shot up two octaves. "I'll run your ass over with a car!"

"I've got this," Derrick insisted again and asked the manager to walk off with him so they could talk without the assistance of the residents.

Jack huddled everyone in the group, including Kat. "Karl has his rope that he uses to rope off his parking spot at the apartment. I say we tie their chairs together and pull them way down the beach."

Before Kat could say anything, everyone in the group agreed, and since Kat knew she would be outnumbered— and the thought that it would make a great story—she went along with it. Jack and Rev. Carter took the rope and started out to the chairs that weren't being attended to while the dispute was taking place closer to the resort. After a short argument of what knot should be used, Jack and the reverend tied a dozen chairs together while Karl slowly crept onto the sand with his golf cart.

Once the final knot was tied, Jack gave Karl the wave to take off. "Here we go!" Karl shouted, gaining the attention of the manager and Derrick. Karl slammed his foot onto the gas pedal and with tires spinning dug a hole in the sand, burying his golf cart and not moving the first chair. "Well, hell." He looked at Jack.

Jack shrugged his shoulders. "It was a good idea." "What are you guys doing?" Derrick walked up looking at Kat, who just innocently smiled. "I've told you guys that these carts will get stuck on the sand."

"No, you didn't!" Karl snapped, mad that his golf cart wouldn't move.

"What did he say?" Rev. Carter pointed to the manager, who was laughing at the failed move.

"He agreed that first come gets the space." "That's our space." Karl yelled from his cart.

"His argument is that we don't use all of our beach space."

"I don't use all my toilet paper in one sitting either, but that doesn't mean someone else can take the rest!" Karl blurted out.

Everyone gave him a strange look over his analogy. "Let's get this unstuck and we'll figure it out," Derrick said.

The life guard from the resort drove their Polaris RZR onto the sand and hooked up to Karl's golf cart. With the accompaniment of spitting orders from Karl, the life guard pulled his cart safely onto the parking lot and drove away.

"That's a nifty cart," Jack replied, watching the life guard speed back to the resort.

Chapter 12

O nce back across the bridge Karl pulled up to find his parking spot occupied by another golf cart, and after a few words and hand gestures, Karl pulled in the spot beside his. "Why didn't you rope off your spot?" Jack asked.

"I forgot, and what would we have used if I didn't have my rope to pull the chairs?"

The five other golf carts filed in their parking spots, and the plotting started before they could leave the area. Ideas from throwing all their chairs and umbrellas into the gulf to turning 10,000 crickets lose in the neighboring resort were tossed around, but it wasn't until a voice with the best idea yet came from the lady wearing camouflage overhearing their conversation—Violet.

"Turn our beach into a nude beach. That would keep them on their side," she suggested, leaning against the building.

"Nobody wants to see you naked!" Karl grumbled. "Exactly! Not that these girls haven't turned a head or two in their day." She lifted her breasts with her hands. "Maybe during the Roman Empire," Karl huffed beneath his breath.

"And we all go to jail," Rev. Carter added.

"I don't know—I think Violet has a good idea," Jack replied. "Let's meet at your apartment in thirty minutes." Jack patted Violet on her shoulder and jogged toward his apartment.

"Where in the hell is he going and what is he up to?" another man said, standing in the group.

"I don't know, but I'll see you guys in thirty. Bring everyone you can," Violet said, walking back to her apartment.

What seemed dramatic, Jack jogged off leaving the rest of the clan to believe he was going to make a plan but his quick departure was only because he had to pee. Thirty minutes later, Jack, Rev. Carter, Karl, and six others met in the lobby of the Tower Apartments to have their meeting about revenge on the resort next door. The elevator doors opened, June standing in the center of the elevator wearing her typical flowery muumuu dress and headband with a single feather hanging from the back.

"Greetings, oh revengeful ones." She waved her right hand.

"And why are we meeting at the Stevens Sisters' apartment?" Karl looked at Jack, who was laughing at June's welcome.

After two dings from the elevator, the doors opened to the Stevens Sisters' floor, and Jack motioned to the door. "Ladies first." He looked at June, then to Karl.

"Oh, haha! Let's get this over." Karl stepped off behind June, followed by eight others.

June opened her door and welcomed everyone in. Karl walked in first, taking four steps before freezing in the middle of their kitchen, followed by Jack who ran into Karl, followed by Rev. Carter, who ran into Jack, and so on. Karl's eyes widened as he tried to catch his breath, looking throughout their apartment at the arsenal that Violet had proudly displayed on the walls of their living room and kitchen.

"Good Lord!" Karl softly claimed.

"What in the hell is this place?" Rev. Carter asked. "I didn't think preachers were supposed to curse?"

Jack said without moving. "We actually get a pass from time to time."

Violet walked out of her bedroom with two pieces of paper. "I printed off an aerial map of the resort." She proudly held up the papers.

"I think I'm out," Karl said, walking to the door, followed by the other men except Rev. Carter and Jack.

"You're too deep in to it now to back out. Stop being a pansy!" Violet cleared a section on their bar to devise their plan.

"Violet, why do you have so many guns?" Jack was the first to ask the question the eight other men were too scared to ask.

"This is nothing. You should see her collection back at home," June smiled.

"Are you sure the death of your attorney was an accident?" Karl asked. The eyes of the other men, who didn't know the story, widened. "And what is that smell?" The spare bedroom door opened, and Simon walked out with a cheerful "Hey, guys!" He looked at Violet, adding, "I've moved everything from the top racks to the bottom; do you need anything else?"

"Nope. Thank you, Simon."

He walked past the men, who had refrozen in their tracks. "Gentlemen," he smiled and walked out.

"We're all going to jail," Karl grumbled.

"What for? We haven't done anything," one of the men said.

"I don't know, I just know we are." Karl gazed back around the room.

"That's wine I smell!" Jack exclaimed. "Merlot?"

"You know your wines," June smiled.

Violet walked over to the spare bedroom and opened the door, exposing 750 gallons of fresh squeezed grapes and boxes of bottled wines and equipment. "Holy Toledo!" Rev. Carter slowly said.

"Is Toledo holy?" Jack mouthed back over his shoulder.

"It is compared to this place."

Karl had turned three shades of white and would have sworn he peed himself, but after feeling his pants, found everything was dry. "I would have taken you as a moonshine gal," Jack replied, peeking in the room at all the carboys full of wine.

"She tried moonshine, but the sheriff kept taking her still. So she settled on wine," June said as if it were normal. "Not just any old wine, chateau!" Violet smiled and poured Jack a sample glass.

He proudly accepted the offer and swirled the wine in the glass like a pro, then took a sip. Looking through the glass at Violet, who was still smiling, he added, "Violet! This is really good." He finished the glass and held it out for another sample. All the other men except for Karl stepped forward for a sample. "I didn't know preachers could drink?" Jack looked at Rev. Carter.

"Something tells me I need to start if I am going to hang out with you guys."

Violet poured everyone a glass, including Karl. "Here," she handled Karl his glass, "you can't back out now; you know too much." She gave him a devilish grin. "You need to sell this," Jack said, looking at his glass. "Oh, she does. She has two gentlemen that come every month and buy cases for their restaurants here in Perdido Key and the next town over," June volunteered the information.

"June! That's not public information." Violet shot her a funny look. The men looked at each other, then back to their glasses, and after sampling two bottles of Violet's finest Merlot wine from the finest grapes of California, the clandestine group of misfits began planning their revenge on the neighboring resort.

Chapter 13

With the time close to 5:30 p.m., "Goodness, it's getting late!" Karl said. "Betty is going to worry that something has happened to me."

"OK," Jack said, "we have our plan." He pointed to Violet, "And Simon is good to go?"

Violet shook her head in agreement and added, "Maybe we should leave in shifts? We don't want to alarm CBC that we're planning something." The group agreed.

"You coming?" Karl held the door for Jack.

"You go ahead; I want to talk to Violet about this wine," he said, still gripping his glass.

"Meet us at supper," Karl replied.

"I'll be right there, I got to stop by Sylvia's first," Jack said. Everyone in the room gave an audible *ohhhh*. "It's not like that," Jack tried to defend himself.

"You can leave the details out. What about my wine?" Violet asked.

Jack waited for everyone to leave, a process that was supposed to be in shifts, but with dinner being served, they either had forgotten or didn't care. "This is some of the best I've had," Jack explained.

"My secret isn't for sale," she smiled.

"Nope, that's not what I am asking. I know some of the main players on the New York City black market wine scene. That is, if you are interested in making some side cash?"

Violet shook her head in thought. "It's not about the money."

"It's about beating the law," June piped up. "Well, either way, you interested?"

"Sure."

"Let me have a few bottles to get to them, and I'll let you know." Jack stood up.

Violet handed him three unopened bottles. "Don't drink them," she said with a nod of understanding from Jack. Jack fetched his straw hat from the kitchen counter and headed straight out to the Loft Apartments to see Sylvia Westheimer with the bottle tucked under his arm. Kat was locking her door to the art center when she noticed Jack nonchalantly strolling into the lobby of the Loft Apartments. Turning to walk to her car, she bumped into Karl. "Karl! You startled me, what's up?"

"He's up to no good." Karl pointed to the door Jack disappeared into.

"I take it a point not to intervene with the love life of residents," she replied with a smile.

"You think he is in love with Westheimer? Hell, she can barely get around."

Knowing this was not a conversation she wanted to have, Kat turned it around. "Where is Betty?"

"Already eating. I'm going in now."

"OK, I better catch up with Derrick." She tried to break away from the conversation.

"You better hurry, I just saw him and Jaqs heading to the parking lot," Karl said, then walked into the café.

"Really?" Kat said to herself, briskly walking to the parking lot. Stepping onto the pavement she caught the taillights of Derrick's truck speeding off down the highway. Steam began building, and Kat's face started to turn red with anger. She pulled out her phone to call Derrick to ask him why he would leave work with the fitness instructor.

"Good evening, Kat." The voice caught her off guard, and looking to her left she caught a wave from Jaqs as she climbed into her red convertible BMW.

"Kat? You there?" A voice on Kat's cell phone snapped her out of her trance.

She put it to her ear, watching Jaqs slowly pull out of the parking lot. "You left without saying goodbye." She gritted her teeth.

"I told you I wanted to run home and clean up before you came over. You are still planning on coming over to watch a movie?" Derrick asked.

"Yes, what do you want me to bring?"

"Nothing." Derrick had a slight pause, "Oh, shoot. I forgot something in my office that Simon was dropping off. Would you grab the paper sack on my desk?"

"Sure." She took a deep breath and thought of their evening and alone time, "So, since there isn't anything I can bring, maybe I should wear something comfortable?" she hinted.

"Whatever floats your boat, see you in ten minutes." Derrick hung up, leaving Kat with a smirk.

"I swear the boy is clueless." She walked to his office and grabbed the paper sack from his desk. After feeling the weight, she looked inside and found an unlabeled bottle of wine. At first thought she wondered what it was, and then thinking that Derrick said Simon had gotten it, she didn't want to know.

After dashing home and changing into something other than work clothes, Kat headed to Derrick's apartment with the sack riding in the passenger seat. Derrick had rented an apartment on the beach only a half mile from CBC after he had taken the assistant director position. Kat pulled up in the parking lot, took one last glance in the mirror at her hair and makeup, then snatched the sack from the passenger seat and headed to the door.

"Can't a lady change and fix herself up?" She smiled. "You looked awesome the way you were." He kissed her, sending a slight spark of electric chill down her back, and closed the door to his one-bedroom apartment, boxes lining the walls with things he hadn't had time to unpack. The sliding glass back door was cracked open, allowing a breeze of salty air to slide inside. Kat could hear the waves washing onto the beach just a short fifty feet from his apartment.

"I take it this didn't come from a store." She held up the sack.

"No." He took it with a flare of excitement. "Simon shared a sample with me, and I'd have to say it's the best wine I've had." He opened the bottle, adding, "Not that I have a great deal of experience with wines."

"Where did he get it?"

"He wouldn't say." Derrick shuffled through the cabinet for a couple of glasses.

"Figures," she replied, looking out at the beach that had already darkened with the sun gone and no moon to show. "You want to skip the movie and sit out on the beach?" She opened the door more.

Clueless about her flirtation motives, "Sure," Derrick shrugged and followed her out. The wind coming from the ocean blew her hair to the side and fighting to get it under control, she glanced back at Derrick. The light behind him defined the muscles that were hidden under his thin shirt, something Kat was hoping he would lose in the near future.

Barely containing herself, she wrapped her arms around his waist and pulled his warm body in to hers. A squealing noise came from the wind. "Was that you?" she giggled.

Shaking his head, he said, "No, sounded like tires." He walked to the side of his deck, where, looking at the highway in front of his apartment, he added, "You're not going to believe this."

Kat had a sense that she would, and in a disappointed tone, said "What?" She joined him just in time to see six golf carts coming down the highway with a half mile of angry drivers behind them. With horns blowing and words being exchanged, Karl led the "Hell's soon-to-be Angels" into the parking of Derrick's apartment.

Karl waved his fist at the first car to speed by. "Up yours! You big A. . ."

Derrick stopped him. "Guys, what in the world are you doing?"

Jack stepped forward, "Need to borrow your truck." He held out his hand for the keys.

Derrick shook his head in disbelief. "Is it legal?" he asked.

"Oh! Hello, Kat." Betty climbed out of their golf cart. "I hope we didn't interrupt your evening." She smiled, cocking her head.

Jack saw the bottle in her hand. "Some good wine," he commented and gave her the thumbs up.

"I haven't tried it yet," she grinned back.

Derrick handed Jack the keys. "Leave it at CBC . . . with the rest of these carts! I'll get Kat to drive me back." Without any remarks, the group jumped back in their carts, followed by Jack in Derrick's truck, and sped off at the high rate of fifteen miles per hour back toward CBC, collecting as many angry drivers as they had when they first showed up.

Chapter 14

An hour later, Violet walked out of her bedroom wearing all black and black makeup smeared under her eyes. "What in the world are you doing?" June asked.

"I told everyone to wear black tonight," Violet replied. "Oh? Did you tell everyone to look like a college linebacker with black under their eyes?" June looked at her oddly.

"That's how cat burglars do it," she smiled.

"I'm pretty sure cat burglars wear a mask," June answered as a knock come from the door. Opening it, she found Jack and five other men, all wearing black. "Oh, good grief! Come in." She shook her head.

"Where is everyone else?" Violet asked.

One of the men stuck his head out the door and hollered in a whisper, "It's clear, come on." He signaled another wave of people to join them along with Karl and Betty.

"What are y'all doing? We are the only ones on this floor." June laughed, then looked at Betty in a black dress. "You always dress up for mischief?"

"It's the only black I have. I only get to wear it at funerals," she explained.

"Which is probably gonna be mine if we get caught! I can't believe you guys talked me into this," Karl huffed. "It was your idea, slim shady!" Violet blurted out.

"Now, where is Simon with the goods?"

A knock came from the door, making everyone freeze. "Oh, for Lord's sake, y'all haven't done anything wrong yet except pick out some ferocious Johnny Cash outfits," June said, shoving her way through the crowd to answer the door. "Speaking of the Lord, it's just the reverend and his better half."

Rev. Carter walked in. "Can anyone tell me why we had to wear black tonight?"

"That's what cat burglars wear, and anyway it shouldn't have been hard for you—don't you do funerals?" Violet said.

"Yes, and by the looks of this crowd, I might be doing more in the near future. But black?" He paused and looked at everyone. "Aren't we going to a resort that is painted all white sitting on a white sandy beach on what will be a full moon night?" Everyone nodded in agreement, "Great! We'll blend right in." He rolled his eyes.

The front door opened, causing everyone to freeze again, but then Simon walked in carrying two uniforms on hangers from the resort custodian's locker room next door. Violet looked around the crowd. "Did you get everything?"

"Yes ma'am, you should have seen the store clerk's expression when I checked out with three pallets of Jell-O and five jumbo boxes of Tide," he smiled.

"OK," Jack started, "Let's go through this again. Simon and one of us, dressed like their custodians, will get their forklift and unload the Jell-O and take it to the indoor pool while the rest of us pour Tide in all their fountains."

"Who is going with Simon?" someone asked in the room.

"It should be Rev. Carter!" Karl blurted out.

Rev. Carter leaned up, "Why?" He looked at Karl who also looked up. "Is it because I'm black?"

Karl felt his blood pressure rise. "No," he choked out. "You're black?" Jack asked.

Rev. Carter looked back at Karl. "You made a reference the other day about watermelon and chicken." He looked at Karl with one eyebrow lifted. "Are you stereotyping me?"

Karl started shuddering. "I wasn't making any "

Rev. Carter started laughing and pointed his finger at him. "Gotcha!"

"If you girls are done with your Black Panther and KKK party, can we get back to the plan?" Violet shot both of them a dirty look.

Jack started back. "OK, Simon and the reverend will get the forklift—"

"We know, we know, you already went over that part," Karl fussed.

"Half of you probably already forgot it," Jack shot him a look.

Betty raised her hand. "I know I did," She said with a smile.

"Drink your tea." Karl rolled his eyes.

"Anyway, once you guys get the pallets unloaded, we should be finished up with the fountains. Once the fountains start spitting out soap bubbles, that should distract them long enough for all of us to pour 1,500 pounds of Jell-O in the pool," Jack instructed.

"Now, remember, if anyone here gets caught, no ratting out anyone else," Violet pointed her index finger at everyone.

"Because catching an old person that can barely move wearing all black isn't going to lead back here to CBC," Rev. Carter replied, rolling his eyes.

After the instructions and a glass of wine, the elvish group made their way to the backside of the property, causing more noise telling each other to hush than a herd of Chinese Pugs. Karl stopped at his golf cart and climbed in, fumbling for his key. "What are you doing?" Violet asked.

"Taking my cart. You don't think I'm going to walk all the way over there?"

"All the way over there, next door? Come on!" she said, following the group to the cinderblock wall that separated the properties. Rev. Carter kissed his wife and told her to be careful, then went with Simon to take Derrick's truck to the loading dock of the resort.

"Isn't this Derrick's truck?" Rev. Carter asked.

"Yea."

"Don't you think the resort will know his truck?"

"Not if no one sees us," Simon answered.

With a big grin, the reverend observed, "We really didn't think this out very well, did we?"

"It will be OK, trust me."

"OK." Rev. Carter climbed in the truck laughing, knowing they were going to get caught, but wouldn't miss it for anything. This is going to make for a great story on my next sermon, he thought as they pulled out of one parking lot and into another carrying 1,500 pounds of Jell-O.

Two security guards sitting in their office not only noticed the suspicious truck pull through the gates, but also the dozen senior citizens all dressed in black disbursing throughout the property. One of them looked at the other. "Should we call the police?"

"Nah, we can take care of a few old people. I wonder what the hell they are up to?" he answered, grabbing a flash light and leaving the comfort of their office.

Chapter 15

Simon backed the truck up to the loading dock and turned off the engine, looking up and down the dark and isolated ally that received most of the resort's supplies from tractor trailer trucks. Simon grabbed Rev. Carter's arm when he opened his door. "Close it, not yet," he said in a soft voice.

The reverend pulled his door closed, causing the interior light to go back off. "What are we waiting for?"

Simon placed his left hand in the air. "Just not yet," he answered, and within moments, two flashlights the security guards were carrying came floating down the alley. Neither paid any attention to Derrick's truck.

"Now, how did you know they would be walking by here?" Rev. Carter asked.

"Not my first time over here," Simon replied. Rev. Carter started to ask another question, but refrained, thinking the less he knew the better. "OK, let's go."

Simon slid out of the driver door and quickly jumped on the forklift.

Rev. Carter nonchalantly walked up and leaned on the fork. "Now how are you going to get this thing started?" he asked, still not convinced they would get away with the prank. Simon smiled, then reached under the seat, pulling out a set of keys. "I don't want to know," Rev. Carter replied with his hands in the air.

"Here," Simon handed Rev. Carter a key card. "Open that door, then the first door to the right—it's the pool door."

Rev. Carter took the card and walked to the loading dock door. "Lord," he started praying, "I'm not sure what I have gotten myself into and I'm sure you do, but when things are all said and done, please make this a story that is believable." He opened the door, then closed it once Simon drove the first pallet in. Looking out the small glass on the door, he saw Jack and two other men run down the alley and continued praying, "Because right now I sure don't believe this is happening."

"Once you're done talking to the big guy in the sky, can you open the pool door?" Simon asked, sitting on the forklift parked in front of the door. After unloading the first pallet, Rev. Carter started to open the door, but noticed through the glass two lights coming down the alley bouncing off the ground and buildings as the two security guards raced by; then he looked back at Simon, who instructed him to open the door.

Once they were in the building with the second pallet, Rev. Carter looked back out to see Karl, June, and Betty run by holding three Tide boxes and Betty carrying her ice tea. Once they had the second pallet unloaded, they had to pause at the door to let the two security guards race by going the other way trying to catch Karl, June, and Betty.

And again, once the third pallet was safely inside, Rev. Carter witnessed Violet, Jack, and others jog by the loading dock. "Why does Violet carry her purse everywhere she goes?" he asked Simon.

"She keeps her .357 magnum in it," Simon answered, not thinking anything of it.

Rev. Carter's eyes grew. "Good Lord, you don't think she'll pull it out on the guards?"

"Hope not. You mind opening these doors again?" Simon answered. And to the surprise of the good reverend, Jack, June, Karl, Betty, his wife, half a dozen seniors, and the gun- toting Violet were inside the pool area, already dumping the 1,500 lbs of Jell-O in the resort's pool.

"How in the world?" Rev. Carter turned and looked back out the door in disbelief that they could have made it inside that quick.

"Come on, reverend, you're in this too deep not to help us," Violet replied. Rev. Carter grabbed a box without complaint, thinking about the purse that dangled from her shoulder.

After a quick fifteen minutes of dumping the Jell-O and cleaning the area of boxes and pallets, Simon said to

Rev. Carter, "I'm going to restart the recording on their cameras; you drive Derrick's truck back, and I'll catch up."

The group had made a plan to separate and make their way back to CBC, so everyone split up and headed back. Karl and Betty walked out through the hallways of the resort and out one of the side doors leading to the parking lot. Only a few steps in the parking lot, a light flashed in Karl's eyes. "Hey, folks, out a little late tonight?" a young security guard asked, smiling that he had caught some of the culprits.

"Late?" Karl asked. The guard shone the light in his face again. "I suggest you turn that light out or you're going to need help from my urologist retrieving it!" Karl barked.

The other guard, showing some reverence, pushed the light to shine on the ground, "Are you folks guests of the resort?"

"Well, yes, why else would we be here?" Karl lied. "And you're wearing black because . . . ?" the guard asked.

Betty and Karl looked at each other, then at the guards. "Funeral." Karl answered at the same time Betty blurted out, "A Johnny Cash tribute." Then they looked at each other again.

The guard cocked his head. "Which is it?" He smiled, thinking he caught them at a lie.

"It's a tribute to Johnny Cash's funeral!" A voice replied from behind the guards, and they turned to see Jack walk up. "Jackson Elbert, suite 508. Now if you two men don't mind, we are already late. Plus I just saw a dozen teenagers run from the front fountain with boxes of detergent in their hands."

The young security guard looked at the older one. "That would explain why we couldn't catch them."

"Sorry to have bothered you folks. Y'all have a good night," the other guard replied, taking off back to the front of the resort.

"Sheeze, I just knew we were busted," Betty commented, following Jack back to CBC. Once back on their property, they broke out into laughter and met the others at the Stevens sisters' apartment, and for the following hour filled the room with loud talking and laughter about their night.

Jack filled the reverend's glass back up with some of Violet's wine. "Well, welcome to our clandestine clan," he laughed.

Karl walked up to the guys laughing. "You are a natural at breaking in," he said, trying to fit in with their conversation.

Rev. Carter looked at him with a straight face. "Because I'm black?" Karl stopped laughing and scrambled for his words, but Rev. Carter went back to laughing. "I'm messing with you."

Next door, the manager and two security guards stood with their hands on their hips, looking at the resort's immaculate indoor swimming pool slowly turn into a solid rainbow block of Jell-O. "And you think a bunch of seniors who need a bridge to get across traffic did this?"

"I swear they looked old."

"But you couldn't catch them?" The manager cut his eyes at him.

The younger guard spoke up. "They were everywhere; it was like geriatric ninjas."

The manager held his hand up for him to stop talking. "And the video footage?"

"Erased."

The manager took a deep breath and closed his eyes, thinking he was either dealing with a clever bunch of seniors or he had hired Barney Fife's cousins. "Get maintenance to clean it up." He walked off.

Chapter 16

Pulling into the employee parking, Kat allowed Jaqs to park her bright red convertible before pulling in beside her with Derrick sitting in the passenger side. He gave Jaqs a small wave as she shut her door, giving Kat the satisfaction of sending a message that he was her man. "Good morning," Kat smiled at Jaqs, who gave her only a slight grin back.

Jaqs, who was wearing aerobic pants and a thin pullover jacket, shed her jacket, revealing a tank top with her dark flawless skin and plenty of cleavage. She walked up to Derrick, saying, "I would like to talk with you this morning about teaching a class on the beach."

Derrick, trying his best to look her in her eyes, said, "Just stop by my office."

Jaqs smiled at Kat and hurried to get in front of them on the walking path. "Don't you think that's a little revealing for a retirement community?" Kat said, feeling her blood start to boil.

Jaqs turned, replying "They're only retired from work, not life." She flipped her long brown hair back over her shoulder and strutted to the fitness studio. And just like the cartoon Peppy Le Pew killing flowers as he walked by them, the senior men of CBC fell into a trance seeing Jaqs walk by.

"Derrick!" Kat said. "What?"

"Aren't you going to say something?" She pointed at Jaqs.

"She's OK, she's a fitness instructor, and they normally dress a little skimpy."

"A little?" Kat stopped in her tracks.

"OK, I'll ask her to have on more clothes when out of the fitness center." He looked over at an elderly man on a bench. "You doing OK, Mr. Jones?"

With a smile a good coroner couldn't remove, "I am now," he replied, holding his chest.

Kat and Derrick stopped in the cross roads of the path, where they both spotted Jack leaving the Loft Apartments and walking their way. "Kinda early to be visiting Mrs. Westheimer," Derrick commented.

"Depends on your definition of early." He smiled and continued walking to his apartment.

Kat looked at Derrick with her head shaking side to side. "I swear, all you men are going to hell."

Another man sitting nearby reading a book replied, "Go to heaven for the climate, Hell for the company." Kat let out a groan and headed to her art studio. "What? Mark Twain said that," the man defended himself.

"I know; for some reason, Kat's not happy this morning." Derrick acknowledged the man.

"Can only be one queen in the hive," he replied to Derrick, then went back to his book.

Without warning, a skidding sound came from behind him, and Derrick turned just in time to see Betty spill her tea over the front of Karl's golf cart. Karl slowly turned his head to Betty, grumbling, "Are we going to have to get you a sippy cup? That's the third time in two days. I'm getting tired of washing this cart."

"You know the rules, you have to stay on the designated path for the golf carts," Derrick reminded him.

"Quit your bellyaching. I brought you your keys. You can't expect me to walk way over here from the cart path." Karl threw him his keys.

Derrick looked behind Karl at the twenty-five feet that separated them from the cart path. "Do I dare ask why you needed my truck?"

"God Lord, Sweet mother of Jesus!" Karl blurted out, seeing Jaqs walking toward them.

Betty set down her tea, exclaiming, "Oh Jaqs, I love that top!"

"Thank you, Mrs. Rutherfurd, I can give you the name of the store I bought it from. You would look great in one."

"How in the world do you keep your skin so soft and shiny?" Betty grabbed her arm.

"She's twenty-eight years old—that's also why she can wear that shirt!" Karl blurted out.

"Are you flirting with me in front of your wife, Mr. Rutherfurd?" Jaqs held Betty's arms and winked at her. "I'm in my mid-thirties," she whispered to Betty, who just laughed, mesmerized by her skin. "And in Brazil, coconut water is the secret. I'll ask the store if they can order some." "Oh, that would be nice." She looked at Karl. "I could brew my tea with it."

Jaqs looked through the golf cart at Derrick. "Could I show you the spot on the beach where I want to teach my class?"

"You're teaching on the beach?" Betty lit up.

"I am, and I expect you to come." She smiled at Betty. "Most of the men couldn't make it through your class in the air conditioning," Karl interrupted. "What makes you think the beach is better? Hell, most of them will stroke out from the sun and heat before they make it to the sand."

"CBC owns 200 feet of beach space, so anywhere is fine," Derrick answered.

"I know, but I would feel better if we look at it together," she replied.

Derrick looked at his office, knowing he had a thousand things to do. "Oh, OK." He set his brief case beside the man reading a book, who for some reason hadn't turned a page since Jaqs walked up. "If you are going to be here for a few minutes," Derrick asked, "can I leave my bag?"

"You and the instructor coming back here together?" "Yes," Derrick replied.

"OK." He smiled.

"Let's go," Derrick said to Jaqs.

Karl grabbed his arm. "Careful, the Devil comes in all forms and fashions."

"Thanks for the advice."

Karl stomped on the gas, sending Betty's tea flying over her right shoulder and making her head bobble back and forth, but with her hair flowing in the wind, she greeted everyone with a big smile and hello. "Oh, look, they are decorating for the Halloween party," she exclaimed while passing the café.

"Bunch of damn pagans," Karl huffed, whipping around the corner to his roped-off parking spot.

Derrick and Jaqs topped the bridge to look out at a peaceful and serine morning. The water was calm with just a small splash of waves on the white sandy beach. She flipped her hair up to feel the breeze coming from the gulf, "What a wonderful day for a walk. Do you want to head down the beach for a morning stretch?"

"I'm sorry, Jaqs. I have a lot of work this morning."

"That's OK." She paused, seeing the manager from the resort next door storming their way, "He doesn't look very happy this morning."

Derrick nodded to the manager, "Good morning."

"Do you know anything about a bunch of criminals trespassing on our property last night and filling our fountains with detergent and turning our pool into a large Jell-O bowl?"

"No, I'm sorry. It is Halloween week," Derrick replied.

"My guards figured it was teenagers, but I have my suspicions."

Derrick shook his head, clueless about the manager's hint. "OK, have you called the police?"

"I think I can handle this myself." He looked at Derrick's right hand where Karl had given him his truck keys back. "Nice shade of purple." He nodded to Derrick's hand.

Derrick looked at his hand, "What in the world is this?" He tried to rub the color off with no success.

"I see how it is," the manager replied and stormed off. "What in the world is he talking about, and why is my hand purple?" Derrick asked Jaqs, who shrugged, clueless as he was.

Chapter 17

C oming out of the bathroom from trying to scrub off the purple on his hands, Derrick was greeted by a gentleman in a uniform shirt holding a clip board. "Can I help you?" Derrick asked.

"I have a delivery for a Mr. Goslin," he said, looking at his clip board.

"Apartment 612 in the Towers," Derrick diverted him.

"I can't take this to his apartment. I'll have to unload it here."

Derrick glanced out the window. "What do you have?"

"His golf cart."

"Why do you have his golf cart?"

"He sent it in for customization." He handled Derrick the clip board for a signature.

Signing the form, Derrick commented, "I thought he already had his golf cart customized from the manufacturer."

"Oh, I doubt they do what we did."

Derrick looked back at one of the assistants working in the office. "Call Jack and tell him his cart is here." He gave his attention back to the delivery guy. "Show me what you did."

They walked out to a four-door, fully customized one-ton truck pulling a trailer with Jack's cart, the decals in the window read "Gulf Coast Choppers." "You guys build custom motorcycles; how did Jack talk you into working on his cart?"

The man looked back at Derrick smiling, "Money talks."

"He had his golf cart enclosed?" Derrick asked.

"Ha, that's not all. Let me show you," the man replied, climbing on the trailer. Opening the door, Derrick peeked in from the ground at the array of gadgets that filled the inside of the cart. Jack had them install a cigar humidifier on the dash, an oak custom glass and bottle holder that was cut out for his favorite bourbon, satellite radio with speakers that lit up with neon lights, mood lights on the roof, and an air conditioner front and rear.

Derrick shook his head. "I do believe Mr. Goslin is spoiled."

"And I should be." Jack walked up, smiling with a gate in his stride. "But the question is, did they install the most important item?" He climbed up on the trailer and looked inside behind the driver seat, then took off his fedora hat and hung it on a brass hook. "Yes, they did."

"Jack, you never cease to amaze me," Kat said, standing behind Derrick.

"Come on, doll, take a ride with me and you'll change your mind about this young lad." He winked at her, opening the passenger door and ready to back it off the trailer.

Once they had backed off the trailer, Derrick started to reach for the back door to climb in the back seat. "Oh no, this ride is just for us," Kat said. Derrick looked at her to figure out if she was kidding or not. "Maybe you should go find your fitness instructor," Kat replied.

Derrick started to say something, but an assistant from the office yelled at him for a phone call. He locked eyes with Kat for a moment before Jack sped off, then walked inside to take the call that was waiting for him.

"Jack, why in the world do you have a navigation system?" Kat pointed to the screen on his dash.

"To drive Karl crazy," he smiled.

"How is that going to drive him crazy?"

"You'll see," he laughed. "You have time to run down to the liquor store?"

"Kinda early," She cut her eyes at him.

"Sweetheart, early left when I turned seventy; now it's just time."

After making the trip three blocks to the store and back, Jack dropped Kat off in front of her art studio for her mid-morning class. Walking in, she found Betty waiting for her. "Where is everyone?" She normally had ten to twelve students.

"They are all going to the beach for Jaqs' new class." "That was quick," Kat said under her breath, strongly disappointed that she was losing people. "Well, we can still get our work in on our paintings. Is that your ice tea?" Kat pointed at Betty's glass, noticing that it reflected a milky swirl.

Betty straightened up. "Oh, yes, I made it with coconut water. I had Karl go to the store for it, but our store here is buying some to carry."

"What has you making tea with coconut water?" "It's the secret the Brazilians use for their skin," Betty whispered.

Kat's expression read her thoughts before she could say it. "Let's me guess—Jaqs told you that."

Betty giggled, "Of course, unless you know of another Brazilian around here."

"No, one is plenty."

"Try it." Betty handed her the glass, then reached in her purse and pulled out a bottle. "Here, put some in a cup."

Kat took a careful sip from Betty's glass and wasn't sure if it was the dislike of Jaqs that made her face wince or the bitter taste of tea and coconut. Either way, it matched Kat's mood toward the new fitness instructor. At the same time, Betty's phone rang loud enough to wake the dead, and she scrambled for it in her purse. "Hello," she yelled in the phone as she always did, not thinking the other line could hear her.

"Good Lord, woman, stop screaming," the voice replied on the other end. Kat could hear Karl's voice just as loud as Betty's. "Come to the beach," Karl said as Betty held the phone away from her head.

"OK, give me just a second." Betty looked at the phone, focusing on the "end" button.

With a disappointed expression, Kat reached for Betty's phone. "Here, let me adjust the volume so you won't bust out your eardrum."

"I have to keep it up to hear Karl."

"Everyone can hear Karl—you're going to hurt your hearing," Kat replied. "This button puts it on speaker so you don't have to destroy your eardrum."

"Oh, I didn't know that." She smiled at Kat. "Thank you, you want to go to the beach with me?"

"No, thanks."

For the first time, Betty saw Kat's expression. "Is it OK that I go?"

"Of course."

"Don't worry, give these folks two to three days and they'll have more pulled muscles and aching bones. Then they'll want to come back to your class to rest."

"Thanks," Kat replied with another grimace. Betty scurried out the door, leaving behind the bottle of coconut water sitting on her table. Kat grabbed it and hurried to the door to give it to her, but Betty was halfway across the bridge. "Coconut water," she said out loud, looking at the bottle. After carefully taking off the cap, she tasted it. "Huh! Not bad." She took a bigger swig.

Chapter 18

After a grueling fifteen minute walk back from the first fitness class, a class that wiped out half of the participants within the first five minutes, June sat on a bench trying to catch her breath. Karl pulled up with Betty in the cart. "You need a ride?" he asked, shocking both her and Betty by his chivalry.

"You only got two seats."

"I can sit in the middle." Betty quickly slid over, giving June room. Karl took off before she could get both feet on the floor, and with the wind hitting her face, she started to cool down.

"I told Violet we need to get a cart, but she insist that we wait," June said.

Karl leaned forward to look past Betty. "Wait for what?"

"She's waiting for the first person who owns a golf cart to die and hopefully buy theirs cheap," June answered.

"She'll probably kill someone first," Karl said, weaving in and around people who were walking on the path and skidding to a stop in front of the café. A bus unloaded a group of elementary children to join the residents for a Halloween lunch and show off their costumes, and they walked in a line past Karl and into the café.

"What's the gaggle of little people for?" Karl asked a teacher that was helping them file into the door.

"We are here to celebrate Halloween with you," she smiled.

Karl's expression went from unhappy to angry. "That's the last thing I want is a bunch of snot nose kids screaming when I'm trying to eat lunch."

"Don't you want to see them in their costumes?" the teacher asked, trying to make light of the conversation.

"No!" Karl didn't give her any room to answer.

Betty whispered to June. "Karl isn't fond of children." "Among all the other ages too," June replied under her breath.

Violet pushed her way through the kids and exited the café with two ice cream cones and a bottle of water sticking out of her pants pocket. "Like wading through alligators with raw meat." She pointed back to the children, who were still eyeing her ice cream cones.

"We better get a seat," Betty said to Karl and June. "I'm not going in there!"

"You need to eat to take your meds."

"Bring me something," Karl huffed, seeing Jack pull up in his new golf cart. "What in the hell is that thing on top of your cart?"

"Part of the AC," Jack smiled, making Karl roll his eyes. "Hop in and go for a ride."

Before Karl could answer "no," Violet piled in the front seat and made a comment about his satellite radio. Karl pulled his cart off to the side, climbed in the back seat, and pulled the door shut. Feeling the cool air, he looked around thinking it was nice to have an AC. Pointing to a small screen on the dash, he asked, "What is that?"

"That's my navigational system," Jack said.

"What in the hell do you need a navigational system for? You won't go anywhere other than the CBC campus and the liquor store."

"Where to?" Jack looked at Violet. "The beach!"

"OK." Jack started to punch in the coordinates. "I think I can press this screen and—"

"Oh, for God's sake, just go!" Karl barked from the back seat.

"Hold your horses. I don't want to get lost," Jack started laughing.

"You probably bought that damn thing just to piss me off. Well, it's pissed me off. Either go, or I'm going to go eat lunch with the lollypop gang."

Jack punched the radio to his new station, New Orleans Jazz, and with all ten speakers blaring out Sidney Bechet and what sounded like a Mardi Gras parade, they headed to the beach a whole 150 yards away. Karl leaned back and put his arm on the head rest of the seat beside him, thinking he could add an AC to his cart. That thought quickly left his mind, though, as they topped the bridge to see the resort next door setting up for a party on the beach, and mostly on their side.

"Why, they're setting up on our side." Karl's voice shot up three octaves.

"I guess the Jell-O and Tide didn't stop them. Head down there!" Violet pulled out her nickel-plated .357.

Jack pushed her pistol back toward her purse as Karl gasped for air from shouting and seeing Violet pull her gun again. "That's why they're setting up on our side. I'm sure they know we did that and this is their way of not backing down. No problem—we just simply show up tonight and crash the party."

"We have . . . ." Karl cleared his throat and started again at his normal tone. "We have our Halloween party." "What time does our party get over? 8 p.m.? They won't even be rolling yet with their party."

"That's awful close to bed time," Karl leaned over the front seat.

Jack turned toward him. "Karl, Gerald's honor is at stake." It was the first time Jack had mentioned his name in a long time.

"OK." Karl got all serious. "For Gerald."

Before they could back down the bridge, the resort's "side by side" ATV came roaring down the beach spraying sand twenty feet behind the treaded tires. "How fast do you guys think that thing will go?" Violet pointed to the ATV. Both men shrugged their shoulders, not knowing and leaving Violet to wonder. Jack backed off the bridge hoping they weren't spotted so that their party crashing that night would be unexpected.

Not wanting the ride to be over yet, they cut through the parking lot, where they spotted Jaqs putting her bag in the back of her convertible. They pulled up beside her, and Violet opened her door, "Hello." Jaqs beat them to the greeting, still wearing her aerobic pants and tank top shirt.

Karl leaned into Jack's ear. "Remember the three things that don't lie? Kids, drunks, and aerobic pants." He giggled, leaning back in the seat.

"How are you guys doing?" Jaqs asked.

"You good at keeping secrets?" Violet started. She smiled, "Yes."

Both men tried to quiet Violet down, "We are crashing the resort party tonight, you want to come?" She devilishly smiled.

"I might be interested," Jaqs grinned.

Violet looked back at the guys. "We bring her, and she'll distract the men while we eat their food."

Jack smiled, "That's a good idea, you in?" He looked at Jaqs.

"Do you think I can distract the guys?"

"Honey, with those girls you can distract most women." Violet pointed to her breast.

Jaqs grabbed both of her breasts, laughing, and said, "I might be able to keep the attention of the men."

"Good Lord! I need a nitro pill!" Karl sucked out most of the oxygen in the back seat.

"Meet us at Violet's before the Halloween party for a drink or two." Jack tipped his hat at her and drove off before Karl went into cardiac arrest.

Chapter 19

People started to file into Jack's apartment by the pairs dressed in their best costumes and bringing their finest hors d'oeuvre. One couple brought fried pickles, which were a big hit and almost gone before Karl and Betty showed up with a good southern pigs-in- a-blanket. Jack walked into the kitchen to greet them, and looking at Karl's lack of costume, added, "Let me guess, you're Karl."

"Dressing up is for children." Karl pulled a Cubs hat from his back pocket. "Cubs fan," he grinned.

"Wishful thinking," Jack answered.

The doorbell rang before Karl could reply, and Jack slid through to open the door to Rev. Carter and Diana, who were dressed up like a priest and nun. "Isn't that cheating? You're already a minister."

"But now I'm a priest!" the Reverend answered with his head turned and a big smile.

"And you are a 1920s gangster?" Diana pointed to Jack.
"Clyde." He held out both arms. "Where is Bonnie?"

"Late, but she'll be here."

They handed him a tray of meats and crackers and joined in with the folks that were already socializing and picking at each other about their costumes. A bottle of Violet's wine, which was now the most popular choice of those who partook in an occasional drink, was opened and quickly evaporated. Jack started to open another bottle when the door opened with June walking in wearing her normal flower child outfit. "I see you didn't dress up either," Karl replied.

"Why, sure I did, I'm a flower child," June answered, not understanding that most if not all the people at CBC had already classified her as the community hippie.

Karl took a swig of his coke, but without warning sprayed it back in his cup and onto two people standing in front of him. "What was that for?" one of the guests said, shaking off the coke from his sleeve.

Speechless, Karl pointed to the door, where standing in the doorway for all to see was a sight that most thought they'd never see . . . Violet Stevens in pigtails, a light blue dress with a white top, carrying a basket, and wearing red ruby slippers. Everyone in the room froze. "What's the matter with all you? Haven't you seen Dorothy from the Wizard of Oz?"

"Not what we expected, and you look great," Betty spoke first. "Don't you think so?" she asked Karl.

"I'll never be able to watch that show again," he huffed, drinking his coke.

Betty popped him on his back, then leaned toward Violet. "We all thought you'd be Jack's Bonnie. What's in the basket?" Violet opened one end, pulling out another bottle of wine, then leaned the basket over to show her nickel-plated .357 resting in the bottom.

Another knock came from the door, and with Violet closest, she opened the door, and again Karl sprayed three others with his coke. Walking in the door was Jaqs, dressed like Elvira with her hair in black, a long flowing black dress, and every bit of cleavage she had showing for all to see. Heartbeats of the men in the room skipped two to three beats, and Violet leaned over to the reverend, saying, "Remember, reverend, you're a man of the cloth." "I'm trying," he mumbled back so Diana couldn't hear him.

"Jaqs, you look exquisite!" Betty grabbed her arm and pulled her in. "I have to confess, I thought you'd be dressed like Bonnie for Jack."

"I might have to do some time travel and leave Clyde behind and join you in the twenty-first century," Jack welcomed Jaqs.

"Jack? Who is Bonnie?" Betty asked, with four other women standing behind her awaiting the answer.

A voice came from behind them, "Why, I am, sugar!" Kat twirled her long pearl necklace around her hand. The room gravitated toward Kat, stealing the attention from Jaqs. "You ready to start our bootlegging operation and rob some joints?" Kat said, smacking on a piece of gum and talking in a 1920's slang.

Violet backed up to Kat. "Quiet on the bootlegging phrases," she whispered to Kat, leaving her to think about the wine collection. Derrick followed, dressed as a 1920's police officer swinging an officer's baton.

Jack held out his arm to escort Kat into the living room. "Come on, Bonnie, the night is young, and we have some partying to do before you're arrested and taken off by the police." He winked at Derrick.

Jaqs slid up beside Derrick. "You can arrest me. I've been a naughty girl," she whispered so no one would hear, leaving Derrick shaking in his stance.

After finishing a few bottles of wine and all the hors d'oeuvres, the group of 18 made a grand entry to the party and dropped their names in the hat for the prizes and costume contest. Kat, who had been dragged all over the party by Jack, finally got to sit by Derrick, who was carrying on a theology conversation with Rev. Carter. "You having fun?" he smiled.

"Yes, you?"

"Of course he is," Rev. Carter shouted over the other conversations. "He's getting a first-class education on why black people stay in church most of the day on Sunday."

"OK?" Kat wasn't sure how to comment.

"OK, folks," a voice echoed from the speakers. "It has been a great night, so before we end, we are going to announce the winner of the costume contest. And just to be clear, employees are not eligible to win," a lady at the microphone replied. "And the winner is . . . Violet Stevens as Dorothy!"

Violet, who was turning red, waved to the crowd in acknowledgment. "Come on up, Violet," the announcer invited.

"I'm good." She refused to go up.

"Come on up, you won a gift card to Walmart!"

Violet shot up from her seat. "I'll take that," she said with a big smile.

"She seems to be overexcited for a gift card," Rev. Carter mentioned to June, who was standing next to him. "She's buying up all the ammo Walmart has," June answered, clapping for her sister and leaving Rev. Carter speechless and worried.

Everyone moved outside and started their journeys back to their apartments—all except the fifteen folks who headed toward the bridge to crash the resort party. And just as planned, they sent Jaqs first to distract everyone as they mingled into the party unnoticed. However, their efforts were cut short when the manager greeted them outside of the roped-off party. "Sorry, folks this is a private party."

"Private? This is our property!" Karl yelled over the heads of everyone.

"No, sir, this is our property and our private party that you folks were not invited to. If you don't leave, I'll have the police escort you back across the bridge."

"You can get all the police you want!" Karl barked back.

"Maybe you should have Dorothy clap her red ruby slippers together and wish you all back safely to your place . . . across the street!" The manager laughed at Violet, whose eyes grew twice the normal size as her face turned beet red.

"You might not want to insult people here," Jack said quietly, putting up his hand.

The manager grinned. "She does look a bit ridiculous, and don't you folks have a bed time?" He turned to walk off, but hearing an unusual clicking sound, he turned to see what it was and was met with the barrel of a nickel-plated .357 stuck within inches of his nose.

His heart missed three beats, and he barely fought off the urge to pee himself. "You want to apologize?" Violet said in a calm voice while gritting her teeth.

"Violet! Don't do anything you'll regret," Betty pleaded with her, then turned to Karl. "Karl! Say something."

With a smirk, Karl said something: "Shoot his ass!" Betty hit Karl with her purse. "Violet, put it down." "Yeah, we'll fix this another way." Jack put his hand on the barrel, lowering the gun and giving the manager a breath of relief. "You might want to leave now," Jack told him.

The manager quickly backed up, knocking over a tray of glasses and stumbling over a couple of guests that weren't aware of the conversation taking place just outside the roped-off area.

"OK, folks, let's take this party back to my place before Violet ends up in the clink." Jack waved everyone back across the bridge. He put his arm around Violet, adding quietly, "I figured Dorothy for a more petite gun."

Still steaming, Violet replied, "Dorothy doesn't play around." She tucked her gun back into the basket.

Chapter 20

At breakfast, the talk was that the resort had run off a dozen residents from CBC beach property and Dorothy had pulled out a .357 and stuck it in the face of the manager. But by the time breakfast was over, the story had grown to Violet shooting the manager and chasing off the rest of the staff. Everyone sat around one table laughing at the expression of the manager and challenging next year's Halloween to be bigger. Rev. Carter and Diana were late and set their trays down at one end; the Reverend looked up at Karl, who was still wearing his Cubs hat, and observed, "Either you slept in that or you partied all night."

"You kidding? The Cubs are on their way to winning the World Series tonight!" Karl piped up, spitting eggs across the table in excitement. "Plus you should be rooting for them, they're God's team."

"Now I know you're going crazy—everyone knows that God's team is the Angels. It just makes sense."

"And that's why they're in the World Series?" Karl smirked.

"Just give it time, baby, give it time." Rev. Carter looked over at Jack. "I figured you'd be in this conversation with your dad playing for the major leagues."

Jack looked at him, wondering where he got the information. "Nah, not really a big fan."

"The son of a major league ball player?"

"Yep," Jack answered, hoping that would end the conversation. Even in his early 80s, the thoughts of his father never being home due to the gruesome travel schedule of a ball player cut deep. Jack thought back to the time when he was 12 and seeing his father come home to his belongings boxed up in the foyer of their home. The echo of his mother's voice explaining that their relationship was over still had the gut-wrenching effect it did 70 years ago.

"Jack?" June tapped him on the arm, pulling him out of his trance. He looked at her, a little confused, as she repeated what she had just said: "Will you pass the salt and pepper?"

"Oh, yea. Sorry." Worried that he wouldn't be able to revisit his memories, he excused himself with "I'll see you guys this afternoon."

Watching him walk off, Rev. Carter asked the table, "Something I said?"

"An absent father leaves deep wounds," Karl replied, taking a bite out of his toast.

"I see," Rev. Carter replied, having lived in the shoes of Jack Goslin.

Jack left his cart at the café and walked toward the Loft Apartments, not realizing that Derrick and Kat were watching from the bench they were sharing. "There goes our village ladies' man," Derrick commented.

"I wish you would have a talk with him," Kat answered.

"None of my—" Derrick stopped and looked at two police officers and the resort manager walking toward them. "Something tells me this isn't good."

"This time your old people have gone too far!" The manager pointed his finger in Derrick's face.

One of the officers pulled his hand down. "I told you we would handle this." He looked at Derrick. "Mr. St. Clair, we have a report that one of the residents of Cedar Branch pulled a gun on—"

"And I am pressing charges. That old bitty is going to jail!" The manager started in again.

"One more time and I am going to have my partner escort you back to the patrol car, understand?" He turned back to Derrick, rolling his eyes. "Apparently this person was dressed up like Dorothy from the Wizard of Oz."

"When? Most if not all our residents turned in after their Halloween party."

"It happened at the resort's beach party last night," the officer answered.

"The party that took place on our property?" Derrick replied, hoping to get the manager rallied up.

"Your old people don't cross that hideous bridge after dark, and I don't see why that is a problem. Plus they poured Tide in all our fountains and turned our indoor pool into a giant bowl of Jell-O!"

The officer turned to the manager. "And you caught them?"

"No, my guards were outrun."

"By a group of elderly people?" The officer lifted his left eyebrow.

"That's beside the point! That wrinkled, overweight hag is going to pay for pulling a gun on me!"

The officer looked at his partner, "Can you escort him back to the car before I lose my cool?"

The other officer walked the manager back to the car kicking and screaming, and Kat spoke up, "It's a good thing you did that; he was about to have 105lbs all over him," she said, steaming.

"Mr. St. Clair, sorry to bother you; one thing I can't stand is disrespect to our elderly. Let me know if this guy bothers you." He put away his notebook and tipped his hat at Kat, "Ma'am."

"Have you ever thought that it seems we are raising a bunch of middle schoolers?" Kat asked.

"Every day." Derrick reached down and locked fingers with her and headed to the café. Walking in, he found the only table that was full was the group he was looking for. They greeted him with their coffee cups in the air, and Betty pulled up an empty chair for Kat to sit beside her. "Anyone here know anything about a gun being pulled on the manager of our neighboring resort?"

It took less than three seconds for the table to burst out into laughter. "You should have seen his face! He almost peed himself!" Violet said.

"Violet, if you can't keep your guns inside, then I am going to have to take them," Derrick replied.

Everyone was still laughing. "Over my cold, dead body." Violet was laughing with the group.

"Please. The police just left, and if the manager hadn't been a jerk, we would be having this conversation at the police station."

"Oh, all right," she answered, thinking that he didn't say anything about her half-dozen collection of Tasers.

"What in the world?" Derrick said, looking over the group and out the window at a truck pulling a trailer with a four-seater ATV that had a three inch lift kit, mud tires, racing stripes, and six large speakers.

Everyone turned to see what he was talking about. "It's here!" Violet shouted. Jumping up and knocking over three chairs and Rev. Carter's water, she hurried outside to meet with the delivery guy.

Derrick looked at Kat shaking his head, but she joined in with everyone who was still laughing.

Chapter 21

Derrick walked outside, leaving Kat with the group of misfits, and paused on the sidewalk watching Violet look over her new toy like a six-year-old on Christmas morning. The first thought that ran through his mind was that CBC was too relaxed on their requirements for the residents' carts, and this was no golf cart, but still fit in the loose requirements.

Now with November on the calendars, Derrick headed back to the office to finish up his plans for the next orientation trip that was scheduled to leave the following day with 8 new residents. It was a larger group than normal, and with the director absent, he worried about their decision on who they were going to leave in charge.

"Good morning," Jaqs said, surprising Derrick as he passed by the fitness center door.

"Good morning. Getting ready for your class?"

"You joining us today?" She smiled, flirting with him.

"Too busy today. Catch up with you later," he answered, stepping back into his stride.

Jaqs leaned around the corner, eyeing him as he walked to the office. "You bet you'll catch me," she grinned.

"He has a nice butt," a voice startled her.

Jaqs looked up to find an older lady struggling with her walker. "Yes, ma'am, he does." She laughed.

Derrick hadn't been in his office three minutes when he heard a roaring noise coming through the walls and closed windows. As the noise and vibration got louder, he raced to the window, just catching a glimpse of Violet and her new 350 horse power ATV fly by with the tires barely touching the pavement. The sight of Violet with her racing gloves, her grey hair flying in the wind, and her WW2 style goggles fitting snug on her face painted the picture of something you would see in a cartoon strip.

Before the dust could clear and Derrick could make it back to his desk, his assistant walked in, saying, "Mr. Rutherfurd is here to see you." She barely got out before Karl shoved his way by her and into Derrick's office.

"That damn woman is crazy! You need to get up and go confiscate that dune buggy from hell! She almost ran over me." Karl's voice grew.

"I will definitely have a word with her." Derrick walked around his desk and escorted Karl back out into the foyer of the offices.

"I would have never moved here if I would have known you let gun totting, fast driving, hillbillies in here." Karl pushed open the door, adding, "I swear!"

And before the door could shut, Violet came racing back by, waving at Karl. "Your golf cart doesn't have a chance," she screamed above the engine.

Karl turned back to Derrick with his blood pressure reaching uncharted numbers. "I promise I'll talk with her," Derrick tried to calm Karl down, but to no avail.

Derrick walked back to his office to a chorus of snickers coming from the women in the office, not how he thought the morning would turn out. Falling back in his chair, he looked at the schedule from the director, a schedule that had changed, leaving him in a dilemma as to who he could leave at CBC while he was on the orientation trip. After contemplating for several minutes, he picked up his cell phone and punched the number for the director.

After three rings she picked up. "How are you this morning?" she asked.

"Oh, you know, normal day here at sunny Cedar Branch. I'm sorry to bother you, but I need to ask you about this next trip." He leaned back in his chair.

"I am the one who needs to apologize. I didn't expect an emergency trip to my parents'. What are your thoughts? Do you need to cancel the trip?"

"No, I'm afraid I won't be able to rebook it for a couple of months. I could just take Simon with me."

"You need a female to go. And you need someone to stay behind to oversee CBC. I don't think you have many options. Take Jaqs with you and leave Kat behind to run the day-to-day operations."

"Jaqs has her classes and—" "She can easily find a sub."

"Kat isn't a direct employee of CBC."

"Trust me, after she landed that money for remodels, the board loves her. If it wasn't for you two dating, she'd be on staff. Take Jaqs."

Derrick took a deep breath. "Kat is going to love this," he accidently said out loud.

"Tell Kat to call me and let me know when you are on the road," the director instructed before the line went dead.

Derrick texted Kat to come by, then tossed his phone on his desk, thinking that this conversation wasn't going to go well. But if I take Simon that might ease things, he thought. And there is always Jack, he did volunteer. He was rubbing his forehead when he heard a light knock on his door, and looking up, he found Jaqs standing in his doorway.

"You look stressed," she observed. "You have no idea," he answered.

"Here, let me do something." She walked behind his chair before he had time to decline her help, and before he could turn away, she had both hands on his shoulders digging in his muscles with her thumbs.

"You don't have to " He tried to stop her, but with the rotation of her right thumb, the tingling shot through his spine.

"You can't deny that this feels good," she said. "No," he stuttered.

After a few minutes of a feel-good painful massage, the tingling slowed down with shots from his spine and a different shot took its place. The shots of daggers coming from Kat's eyes as she stood in the doorway. "Maybe I should come back at a better time?" A strong hint of anger cracked in her voice.

"Maybe so." Jaqs sent back a devilish grin.

Derrick shot up from his chair like a bomb had just gone off in his office. "No, she was, I mean I was—"

"I was just leaving." Jaqs strutted to the door. "Come by my studio and see if I can work out the tightness in your shoulders." She looked at Kat, adding, "You can come by too."

"No, thanks." She watched Jaqs leave, then stepped into Derrick's office, pulling the door closed behind her. Derrick struggled, swallowing.

"Really?" she started.

"She started before I could stop her."

"Right! You looked so distressed," Kat answered.

He tried to put his arms around her, only to be pushed off. "I'm sorry. It won't happen again."

"Better not! What did you want to talk to me about?" Kat asked, seeing Derrick's complexion turn white.

Chapter 22

In a light jog, Kat made her way through the courtyard with blurry vision from the tears that filled her green eyes. Praying that nobody would see that she was crying, she quickly made her way to her car, not sure if she was mad or hurt. The news that she was asked to oversee CBC while Derrick was on his orientation trip was exciting and honorable, but learning that he had chosen Jaqs to go with him was more than she could bear. Dropping her keys twice before she could find the ignition just aggravated her even more, and now with the phone ringing in her bag, she just lost it.

Screaming and beating the steering wheel just couldn't make it go away, so she took a deep breath and started her car and drove to her condo. Her phone rang again, but this time she turned it off without looking at the screen. She knew it was Derrick and wasn't interested in hearing his explanation.

She pulled into her familiar parking spot that took only two minutes to reach from CBC and glanced up at her balcony, then at the paved trail that ran adjacent to her building. The trail had been developed years earlier by the city council to join the community and to encourage exercise. Kat started down the trail heading opposite from CBC, but after making it a half mile, she sat on a beach and buried her face in her hands.

She could hear the footsteps of people passing by and some even slowing down, perhaps trying to find the courage to ask her if she was OK, but no questions were ever asked. Then in the distance, she could hear people yelling, but she couldn't make out what they were saying. Not caring, she kept her face buried in her hands until the sound of tires on the pavement stopped in front of her.

She looked up to see Jack's golf cart. "Hop in!" he said, with Dean Martin playing in the background.

"What in the world are you doing?" she asked, confused that he had driven from CBC to her condo. "And how did you know where to find me?"

"Hop in," he repeated.

Without arguing, she climbed in the golf cart, and before she could close the door, Jack sped off. "Did Derrick send you?" she asked, thinking he wouldn't have had enough time.

"Nope, saw you getting in your car upset. What's the matter?"

She pointed ahead of them at a couple walking, "Watch out!" Jack swerved around the couple, escaping with only a few choice words coming from the man. "You know you're not supposed to be on the trail with your cart," she chided him.

"Don't avoid the question."

"I don't know, I am probably over reacting." She took a deep breath and wiped her eyes. "Derrick is taking Jaqs on the orientation trip this week, and I know how she feels about him. I don't trust her."

"And you're mad at Derrick about her trust?"

"No, he could have picked anyone but her. Seems he likes the thought of her flirting with him." She grabbed the door as Jack swerved around another person.

"I think everyone likes the thought of being flirted with."

"That sounds like something a man would say," she replied, still mad.

"That's not a man thing," Jack answered. "Men just think about themselves." "That's not true," Jack defended himself.

"Hell, you've been entertaining Sylvia for weeks now," she said, "and who's that for?" The words left her mouth before she realized what she was saying.

Jack slammed on the brakes and shifted in his seat to look at her face to face. "I understand you're mad right now, and I can take it. But you need to look at yourself, and I mean take a deep look! I don't know who hurt you in the past, but Derrick St. Clair is a soft-hearted man that adores you! And trust me, there is a huge deference in somebody liking you over somebody that adores you."

Kat just stared at him with no expression. "I've had five wives, four that I loved, but only one that I absolutely adored. So until you figure out a way to allow Mr. St. Clair to break down this wall you've built, be prepared to throw more fits and be upset."

Jack started back toward Kat's condo. The ride back was silent, with Kat in deep thought about what she had just heard. "So I'm over reacting?" she asked.

"I wouldn't say over reacting, but I would put yourself in his shoes. He does have people helping him make his decisions, and I mean people telling him what to do."

She looked at his cigar humidifier, air conditioning, custom bottle holder, and the navigational system. "Good advice coming from a man that over kills his golf cart accommodations," she smiled.

"Over kill?" He laughed. "Just living life. Now off you go." He leaned over and opened her door.

"Gee, a gentlemen would walk me to the door." She tried to make the situation light.

"Oh contraire, a true gentlemen never walks another man's girl to the door."

"Thanks, Jack, you are a true hero." She kissed him on the cheek and stepped out. "I'm sorry for what I said earlier. I'm sure what you and Mrs. Westheimer have is special."

Jack gave her a grin and wave, pulling the door closed and starting back on his two-mile trek back to CBC. Thoughts raced through his head about Sylvia Westheimer and his special relationship he had with her, a relationship that nobody knew about. He knew that Sylvia was a social media guru from hearing her talk in the café, and one day, after her table of people had cleared out, he asked her for a favor that had been tugging at him for many years. With her giving heart and excitement to help others, she gratefully obliged his needed research— to find his first love and the woman he adored, Delilah.

Chapter 23

Derrick walked along the parking lot designated for the residents' golf carts. There were a few carts with simple amenities, then Jack's cart that looked like something off the movie Caddy Shack and Karl's plain cart with no frills and two orange cones marking his spot. Then there was Violet's ATV, and Derrick shook his head at her latest addition to her machine, a license plate that read Bite Me. As he started to walk off, something caught his attention that was out of the ordinary, a chain that ran through Violet's left front tire and around the golf cart parking sign.

Derrick picked up the lock that linked the chain together. "Karl is biting off more than he can chew," he said to himself, and before he had time to stand up, a voice caught him off guard from behind him.

"Did Rutherfurd do that?"

Derrick turned to find Violet standing behind him wearing a white helmet with a tinted front glass covering her face. "Violet?"

She pulled the helmet off. "Who were you expecting?" "Did you trade in your goggles for a racing helmet?" "June insisted." She walked around him, then opened

a box mounted in the back of her ATV and taking out a set of bolt cutters. "Watch out, junior!" She pushed him to the side.

"Do you always travel with bolt cutters?" he asked, amazed at her readiness.

"You never know when you might need them," she replied just as the lock snapped in half from the force of the cutters.

"Violet, the purpose in allowing golf carts on the property was to allow residents to travel to and from the beach in a slow and safe manner."

Holding her helmet under her arm, she replied, "What's your point?"

Knowing this was a conversation he wasn't going to win, he asked instead, "Just please go a little bit slower around the property."

"If I wanted to go slower, I would ride with putts." She pointed to Karl's cart.

"Please."

She pushed her helmet over her head with a cynical laughter. "OK," she replied with her voice muffled by the helmet, and climbed in her ATV, firing up the engine and drowning out any other remarks that Derrick might make.

Derrick gathered up the chain and cut lock and headed to Karl's apartment. After a few questions from residents about the lock and chain, he stepped in front of Karl's door, knocking lightly. The door swung open with Betty smiling holding a glass of tea. "I told him not to lock her cart. You can put it there in the corner." She pointed to a corner in the kitchen, "He's over at Jack's."

"Thanks." Derrick stepped out and knocked on Jack's door, and after a shout from inside he entered. "Gentle—" He paused and saw the smoke coming from the balcony. "Jack. You can't use your grill on the balcony."

"He's not." Karl defended Jack. Derrick pointed at the smoke rolling into the wind. "That's the George Forman grill we bought."

"A grill in a grill."

"Nope, that there is an indoor grill and meets the safety requirements to be on the balcony," Karl proudly announced.

"Doesn't cook like my other grill, though," Jack said, snipping the end of a cigar with a silver pair of cutters.

Karl happily unfolded the notice about no grills allowed that was put out by CBC. "Says right here no gas or charcoal grills allowed. It doesn't say anything about electric grills!" He smiled and folded the paper back up and put in his front pocket.

"Fine, you win," Derrick replied.

"Damn right we win." Karl walked back out on the balcony, followed by Derrick and Jack. The sound of Violet's engine roared through the buildings before her

ATV appeared rounding a corner and flying across the bridge. "How did she get her hell machine cut loose?"

Derrick handed him the cut lock. "You shouldn't lock up people's rides, especially Violet's."

"You cut my lock?"

"No, Violet did." Derrick answered, watching two people jump out of the way of Violet's ATV as she sped down the beach.

"You're going to leave Kat with her hands full when you go on this trip," Jack said before he realized he shouldn't have.

"How do you know that Kat is in charge while I'm gone?" Derrick asked.

"He saved you by talking to her earlier," Karl replied.

Jack swatted him with an oven mitt. "Don't tell him that!"

"You talked to Kat?" Derrick asked, confused.

Jack took a deep breath. "I saw her jump in her car crying, and I followed her to her condo and talked to her."

"What did she tell you?"

"Just that you were taking Jaqs with you on the ordination trip."

"Damn good marketing move, I must say," Karl said, lifting the lid to the grill and checking their steaks.

"It's not a marketing move. I don't have much choice. I better get a glass." Derrick helped himself to Jack's bourbon. "I don't know what to say. She has no reason not to trust me."

"Ha! Her last boyfriend is in jail for attacking her," Karl blurted out.

"And taking a Brazilian beauty who flirts heavy with you doesn't help either," Jack added.

"I'm taking Simon too," Derrick replied. Both Jack and Karl cut their eyes at him. "What do you think I should do?"

"Sitting here with us is definitely not the answer," Jack said.

"Yea, get your ass over there." Karl pointed in the direction of Kat's condo.

"How do you guys know where she lives?"

"Phss, please. We know where everyone lives," Karl replied.

"Even Jaqs?" Derrick asked, and by the smiles on their face, he got his answer. "I'll go talk with her, but I still don't know how I am going to handle her when I'm on this trip."

"Call her every waking minute," Jack answered. "How many men are going on this trip?" Karl asked. "This is a unique trip. Four widowers and two couples."

"Those poor bastards are going to stroke out the first time they get pool side with Jaqs." Karl lifted the steaks off the grill.

Chapter 24

Violet topped the bridge linking the community to the beach, never letting off the gas and jumping the parking curb onto the white sand.

A few residents watched as she drove onto the wet sand caused by the crashing waves and headed toward the resort's property. After watching Violet driving up and down the beach for a few minutes, a disgruntled guest of the resort stormed up the beach and called the resort's security office from a phone on their walkway. With the response time of most fire departments, the security guards raced onto the beach with their ATV and chased down Violet, cutting her off and causing her to stop.

Removing her helmet, she greeted them with "Howdy, boys!"

"If you don't keep that ATV off our property, we will be forced to call the police!" one of them demanded.

Violet looked toward the road examining what part of the beach she was on. "According to that fence, we are on CBC property. So you need to get your prissy white asses off our property!" She smiled.

"I'm not sure why you old people think you can run the world—"

"Probably because we do," Violet interrupted him. "You need to get that machine off the beach, now!"

He raised his voice.

Violet smirked, thinking about how long she'd spend in prison if she dragged this guy out of his ATV and ran him into the Gulf of Mexico . . . at gun point. "Because I'm in a good mood, I'll let that slide, and the fact you don't know me."

"I know who you are, and you probably have that gun you pulled on our manager, but I'm not scared of an old lady."

Now prison didn't seem so bad to Violet, and before the security guards had time to react, she pulled out her favorite nickel-plated .357 and took aim at their front right tire. After the smoke cleared and the sound came back, the security guard in the passenger side fell out of the ATV, not knowing whether to run or take cover behind their ATV. The driver miraculously gained manners and a nicer tone.

"Now, the fact is, if you call the police, they'll take my gun and probably put me in the clink for a day or two. In which case, when I get out, I will find where you live and make sure you don't pass your rude manners to any kids you might think about having." She aimed the gun at his crotch. "What's it gonna be? Leave me alone? Or walk funny for the rest of your life?"

Without answering, the driver put their ATV in reverse and drove backwards to their side of the beach and toward the resort, leaving the other security guard exposed to Violet and the shine that reflected off the barrel of her pistol. "You need something?" she asked.

"No, ma'am." He turned and ran after their ATV.

Violet laughed and put away her gun. Seeing her sister walking across the bridge, she drove back to the parking spots and turned off her ATV.

"I thought I heard fireworks," June commented. "Kinda. Just teaching our youth of today a few things about respect."

"Well, you are here just in time for a sunset." June reached out and took Violet's hands and pulled her onto the beach.

"I don't know what is so important about a sunset," Violet tried to resist.

June looked at her with a smile. "We don't have many left."

"I bet there are a lot of sunsets in heaven," Violet grumbled.

"If you keep pulling that gun out, you are not going to find out if there are sunsets in heaven."

"Whatever." Violet followed June closer to the water to find a seat in the sand. They watched as the sun descended into the west while people walked up and down the beach tripping on the ruts left by Violet's ATV. With a light wind blowing from the gulf, the sisters never heard the man that walked up behind them, but sensing somebody there, June turned around to find the resort's manager.

"Well hello, did you come to join us for the sunset?" she asked.

"I would love to," he sat down in the sand. Violet leaned past June to look at him, but he stared into the gulf. "Beautiful day," June observed.

"It is. You might want to be careful with your ATV here on the beach. My security guards ran over something that caused a flat tire," he said, still looking at the gulf.

"Oh, I'm sorry to hear that. But we don't drive on the beach. It's illegal." June smiled at him, not having a clue what he was talking about.

"It is illegal," he replied.

"Then why does your staff drive on the beach?" Violet asked.

"We have a permit and purpose."

"Is policing part of your permit and purpose?" "It is on our own property," he answered.

"And where did your security guards come up with this flat tire?" Violet stared at him.

He shook his head then looked at her. "I don't believe we have properly met." He reached out to shake her hand. "My name is Hank."

June beat Violet to his hand. "Hi, Hank, I am June, and this is Violet."

"You know, you remind me of our attorney back at home," Violet said, shaking his hand and eyeing him down.

"Your attorney back in Camden, Arkansas," he replied.

June looked at him surprised. "Why, yes. How did you know where we lived?"

"I know a few things, like how your attorney died in your house falling through the floor. Mysterious freak accident, wouldn't you say?" He looked at them.

June's eyes widened as she looked at Violet. "Yep," Violet answered calmly on the outside and shaking on the inside.

"I also know that our local police will side with the residents of CBC almost every time there is an incident. So no need for me to call them. But!" He looked back at the sun that was dipping into the water. "I'm sure there is more to the story. So, enjoy the sunset." He stood up and dusted off his slacks.

"Stay on your side." Violet looked at him, not backing down.

He smiled, said "Ladies," then walked back to the resort.

Once he was out of hearing distance, June turned to Violet. "How in the world would he know that?"

"Probably police reports. I'm not going to be threatened like that." She watched him disappear around their outdoor pool.

"You need to lay low and stop causing issues with them," June said.

Not taking her eyes off where he disappeared, Violet replied, "OK," but in a not-so-convincing tone.

Chapter 25

Karl held open the door to the social center for Betty and her ice tea, and four more people dashed through the door before Karl could enter. A little old man nodded toward Karl. "Thank you," he replied.

"I'm not the damn greeter," Karl huffed and stepped in before three women made it to the door. The room was filled with several people who had gathered for the traditional game night. Karl slipped out of his navy wind breaker and threw it across a chair next to Betty's ice tea glass, then scanned the room, thinking she had quickly disappeared. Her small frail hand waved at him while she stood in front of the Rev. Carter and Dianna.

"Preacher," Karl acknowledged him with a grumpy voice and a nod.

"Sinner," Rev. Carter answered in the same tone.

Karl's head shot up. "Sinner?" His voice climbed two octaves.

Laughing, the Reverend replied, "I'm teasing you. We missed you this past Sunday."

Karl looked at Betty. "What was this past Sunday?" "Service," Rev. Carter answered for her.

"Service?" Karl looked at Rev. Carter. "I've been going to church my whole life, and I've heard the same story over and over again. Trust me, I get it. You need to focus on people like those hell-bound, gossiping old biddies." He pointed to a group of women.

Rev. Carter folded his arms. "Because judging isn't a sin."

"Nope! The Apostle Paul told the Chinese in the Book of Acts that judging one another would keep them in line." Karl straightened up with a smile on his face.

"Huh, and where in Acts does it say that?" "I don't know. I read it on the internet."

"And if it's on the internet, it's got to be true?" "Well, yea. There's even a damn commercial to back that up. How are you preaching if you don't know these things?"

Before Rev. Carter could answer, a lady announced over the speakers for everyone to take their seats. Diana pulled Rev. Carter toward their chairs across the table from Karl and Betty. "Dianna, that man is crazy if he thinks Paul was in China. I need to—"

"Not now, honey. Let it go so we can have a great evening."

Rev. Carter tried to argue his point to both his wife and to Karl, but was asked to quiet down by the lady on the microphone so game night could start. He folded his arms and slumped back in his chair, pouting.

"OK, everyone. Y'all ready for game night?" the lady excitedly announced. "I'm going to turn it over to our guest MC for the night, Simon!" Everyone who heard her clapped.

"This ought to be interesting." Karl rolled his eyes, looking at Rev. Carter.

"China? Really?" he said to Karl with Dianna elbowing him in the side.

"Hey, everyone." Simon waved at the crowd speaking slow and loud in the microphone. "Who is ready to play trivia?"

The lady standing beside him covered the microphone with her hand, telling Simon something. "Why in the hell is he yelling in the microphone?" Karl leaned over to Betty. "And why would talking slowly make it easier to hear him?"

"Now, now." She patted his leg. "Idiot!" Karl grumbled.

Simon gained control over the microphone again. "I thought it would be fun to jump back in time and have a 1990s trivia game."

An elderly man from the front row, replied, "Son, we were old in the 90s too."

Simon smiled. "OK. Everyone get in groups of four for teams," he instructed them, and after 15 minutes of folks arguing and swapping seats, the teams were formed.

Karl, Betty, Diana, and Rev. Carter were sitting together as their team. Karl whispered in Betty's ear, "Why did you pick the Carters? He doesn't even know his Bible."

"OK." Simon started, "Who is the number-one boy band?"

A light grumbling came over the crowd, with half of them trying to figure out what a boy band was and the other half still arguing over the teams. A lady yelled from the back of the room, "The Beatles!"

"No, I'm sorry. It wasn't the Beatles." Simon answered, then looked at the other teams.

"Why?" someone else yelled.

"We are looking for the number one boy band in the 1990s," Simon answered.

Another voice shouted from the front of the room, "The Monkees!"

"No, the 1990s!" Simon spoke in the microphone. "The Osmonds?" the same person asked.

"No, it has to be from the 1990s," someone else yelled across the room. The crowd broke out into an argument about whether the Monkees were still together in the 1990s and if a Barbershop Quartet counted. Simon quickly lost control and was desperately trying to regain the audience while talking in the microphone, but was greatly drowned out.

Karl stood up and yelled for everyone to shut up, and after everyone quieted down, "For the love of Pete! It was the Backstreet Boys!" Then he sat back down.

"Yes!" Simon yelled and pointed to Karl, then turned to the lady standing next to him. "Karl sure talks a lot about the love of Pete. Who is Pete?"

"How did you know that?" Rev. Carter cocked his head at Karl.

"Anyone with a half brain would know that." For the next 30 minutes Karl astonished everyone with his knowledge of the pop culture of the 1990s, and their team swept the game with 21 right answers.

Betty put her arm around him. "My encyclopedia."

After the night was over, everyone was filing out the doors heading toward their apartments. "Rutherfurd?" Rev. Carter asked, "You coming to service this Sunday?"

"Depends on what you're preaching on."

"The sanctification of the Apostle Peter and his death for the gospels," Rev. Carter proudly answered.

"Peter? He was the Australian that betrayed Jesus," Karl replied. Rev. Carter just stood there with a blank stare on his face. "I'm just messing with you," Karl slapped him on the shoulder. "We all know that Peter helped Martin Luther King Jr. with desegregation." He grabbed Betty's hand and walked off.

Rev. Carter looked at Diana, shaking his head. "Is he serious?"

Rounding the corner to their apartment, Betty said, "You shouldn't mess with the preacher like that."

"What fun would church be if you can't mess with the assistant boss?"

"Assistant boss?"

Karl pointed up with a grin. "He's the big boss."

Chapter 26

Derrick pulled up to the cedar-sided condos that were less than a couple of miles from CBC and Kat's home. Turning off the key, he mumbled to himself, "Don't screw this up." He walked up to the door and lightly knocked in a familiar rhythm that Kat would recognize, and after a short moment he heard her footsteps coming. The door swung open with Kat standing in the doorway, and even though she was only dressed in shorts and a t-shirt, a lump formed in Derrick's throat. Once he managed to swallow, he said, "Hey, have you got a minute?"

She stepped to the side, saying "Come in."

It wasn't the warmest greeting, but he wasn't expecting her to throw herself at him, either. She walked past him, returning to her sofa and TV show. "If you want something to drink, it's in the refrigerator."

"Jack told me he came by."

Rolling her eyes and shaking her head, she replied, "Of course he did," secretly hoping Derrick had come on his own.

Picking up on her sarcasm, Derrick added, "I was coming anyway to check on you." He sat down beside her, "I'm sorry. I didn't expect Jaqs to jump behind me for a massage."

"It didn't look like you were fighting her off, either." She looked at him.

"No, I guess not. I am not in the least bit interested in her, please understand you have nothing to worry about. Her or anyone else. I think you are—"

"Don't dare say I am over reacting!" She glared at him.

He paused, and even though her eyes shone with anger at him, they were still the most beautiful eyes he had seen. "I wasn't going to say that. I think you are the most beautiful girl and any guy who would jeopardize his relationship with you would be a fool. I'm not going to be that fool." Kat shrunk in the sofa a few inches, feeling both guilty and giddy. "Kat, I love you, and nothing is going to come in between that."

She took a deep breath and then threw her arms around him, causing him to fall back on the couch, then climbed on top of him. "Damn you, Derrick St. Clair. Why do you have to be so charming? Can't a girl stay mad at you?"

He smiled. "Nope, never had that problem."

Playfully punching him, she rolled off and headed toward the kitchen, calling out, "Do you want something?" She grabbed a bottle of water.

"Yes. Let's go for a walk." He pointed at her sliding door that led through her balcony to the beach.

One good thing about living on the beach was that you never need to put on shoes to walk, and after Derrick shed his, they walked out into a cool breeze that rolled off the gulf. Staggering through the soft white sand, they made it closer to the water and walked on the moist sand, holding hands in the night air. With a few warm hellos from northern snowbirds walking past, they stopped at a set of wooden beach recliners forgotten from the day. Derrick pushed two of the chairs side by side for the two of them to watch the waves roll in with a backdrop of stars.

Kat slid off her chair and curled up next to Derrick. "Can't believe you are leaving in the morning."

With his arm around her, Derrick replied, "I'm not going to be gone long, just a week."

"Still."

"Plus you have the whole place to yourself. Miss Boss." He chuckled.

"Yeah! I get to manage not only the employees, but a winery," she replied sarcastically.

Derrick laughed. "Don't worry, everyone loves you. You'll do great."

"Are you sure you don't want to take Violet? She could help you with the seating arrangements." Kat giggled.

A gust of wind kicked up sand, blowing it across the couple, and Derrick pulled Kat in closer to shield her. "Wow, where did that come from?"

"God," Kat softly replied with a tingling covering her body from Derrick's arms holding her. Kat drifted off in thought about how the last year had gone. It was a whirlwind of events, from falling in love with Derrick, to her ex-fiancé stalking her, to Gerald passing away and leaving CBC a handsome amount of money. "Derrick?"

"Hmm?" He answered in his own trance. "Where do you see yourself in three years?" "Why three years?"

"I don't know, 3, 4, 5"

"Hopefully here with you on this beach," he replied, trying to be slick.

"I mean, what about your dreams?" "I don't know, what about you?"

Kat smiled thinking about her childhood dream, "I hope to have my own art gallery and have traveled through Europe. I've never been to Paris, and that is on my bucket list."

"Europe? I wouldn't have picked you as a traveler."

Disappointed in his response, she replied, "Well, it is just a dream."

Picking up on her tone, Derrick backed up. "I don't mean it like that. Chase your dreams, you only live once."

He paused, "My dream would be to own a charter boat in the Virgin Islands."

She leaned up and looked at him, "A boat?"

"I like entertaining, and if I can survive CBC and everyone that lives there, I can survive 4-6 people for a week at sea."

Lying back down, she said, "That's an expensive dream."

"It's just that, a dream. Hey, I know. We open an art gallery on a boat in the Virgin Islands."

Kat laughed. "Yeah, that would work." She drifted back off to her thought and lost all track of time. Before they realized it, the beach was empty from the snowbirds, with only a few lights from the resorts reflecting off the sand.

Chapter 27

The following morning, Derrick finished packing up a few things in his office for the orientation trip. He yawned, thinking that his late night with Kat probably wasn't the greatest idea before a week- long, restless trip. Kneeling down on one knee behind his desk, he was shoving a handful of files into his bag when a thud startled him, and looking up, he saw Kat dropping her bag on his desk. "Moving in already?" he asked.

Kat jumped and let out a squeal. "What in the world are you doing, trying to scare me?"

"No, I'm gathering my files from my desk."

"Correction, my desk." She smiled, then walked around the mahogany desk to move in for a morning kiss. "Last night was fun."

Before he had time to answer her or get that morning kiss, a voice from the door interrupted them. "I don't mean to break up a good kiss, but where should I put my bags?" Jaqs asked.

With a disturbed expression, Kat said under her breath, "I'll tell you where to put your bags."

"Just put them outside the door and we'll load them later," Derrick answered. "We need to get in the meeting room to welcome our new residents." He leaned back to Kat and pecked her on her lips, leaving all the romance for another time.

"So, Kat. What are you doing while I have your boyfriend for the week?" Jaqs asked with a cynical smile. "Rewriting our hiring policies to make sure we hire people with professional appearances," Kat answered with one hand on her hip.

"I agree. It's a good thing I'm a fitness instructor, or I might be violating this new rule." She turned to walk out, and looking at Derrick, added, "Among other things" in a lower voice.

Derrick, not hearing her remark, looked at Kat. "I wish you would try to get along with her."

"Are you serious?"

A knock came from the doorway. "What are we going to call the trip this week?" Simon said in his surfer accent.

"How about 'orientation trip?'" Kat answered.

"You take all the fun out of it. I'll converse with Jaqs." Simon left disappointed.

"You need to lighten up." Derrick smiled.

They walked out together and after a few instructions for the assistants in the office, Derrick and Kat filed in the meeting room that already had filled with new residents and old ones too. Karl had already struck up a conversation with a gentleman who obviously couldn't get a word in on their conversation. Betty was busy introducing herself as if she were running for office along with her ice tea. The door flung open, and Violet strutted in like a four- star general wearing a leather bomber jacket and white scarf and carrying her helmet. "Look, honey, your luggage loader and seat assigner is here." Kat smiled at Derrick.

"Thanks."

"Folks." Derrick said trying to rally the troops. "I'd like to welcome you to Cedar Branch. My name is Derrick St. Clair, and I will be leading your trip along with two of my co-workers. This is Simon, who works in the independent living here at CBC." Derrick pointed at Simon who took a theatrical bow. "And this is Jaqs, our fitness instructor."

"Holy cow!" the man that was listening to Karl replied.

Karl blocked his mouth with the back of his hand. "Pace yourself," he said to the man.

"I can assure you this will be a great week," Derrick continued.

"Where are the Carters? Aren't they supposed to go?" Karl asked Derrick.

"They are going to catch another trip—he wanted to preach at the church service," Derrick answered.

"He can still go and make church," Karl said, then turned to Betty. "Why doesn't he want to go?"

She patted him on the side. "I don't know, sweetheart."

Turning back to the crowd, Karl added, "Well, it was the best damn week we've had since moving in here," he announced. "Except someone died!" he added.

Derrick nervously laughed, "Anyway, let's have a seat and introduce one another." He motioned for Kat to escort Karl and Betty out before Karl tried to help again.

Kat grinned, "What? You don't want the Rutherfurds to assist?"

"Please. And Violet." He pointed.

But before Kat had a chance to corral Violet, she pulled up a seat beside Jaqs and sat with her helmet in her lap. Kat whispered in her ear, "Let's give them an opportunity to meet one another."

"I will." Violet folded her arms, not understanding that Kat wanted her to leave. But with Karl and Betty looking for chairs to join the group, Kat had to leave Violet behind and usher them out the door.

After going around the circle letting everyone tell who they were and where they came from, Derrick started to explain their day when a lady interrupted him. "You didn't let her introduce herself." She pointed at Violet.

"Oh, don't mind me. I live here, just wanted to make sure we weren't getting any liberals!" Violet smiled at the lady.

Derrick felt a bead of sweat form on his forehead. "She's our village jokester." He laughed, trying to play off the remark.

"Jokester?" Violet answered, then looked at the crowd. "If you need a good bottle of wine or a reliable side arm, I'm your gal!" She pointed her thumb at herself. "OK!" Derrick shot up from his seat. "Let's take a tour of the facilities." Everyone stood up and gathered at the door. "Violet, thanks for stopping by. I need to show these folks around," he desperately tried to hint. Violet just looked at him.

"Sweetheart, do you mind if we can just show the new residents the area?" Jaqs put her hand on Violet's shoulder.

"Sweetheart? Save the smooth talk for the men." She looked at Derrick, adding, "Why didn't you just say so, slim?" She voluntarily headed out.

"Slim?" Derrick shook his head.

Just as everyone gathered outside, Derrick heard Violet fire up her ATV. Crap! he thought, and then witnessed Violet flying by in a dust cloud with helmet on and white scarf flapping in the wind. A gentleman turned to Derrick. "Do we all get one of those?" He smiled.

An hour later, as the group was walking through the ice cream parlor of the general store, Rev. Carter joined the group. Just as any good preacher, he politicked the whole time they walked back to the meeting center. Under the canopy where the van was parked, Derrick noticed that Karl and Betty were back, and walking around the van, he found Violet ordering Simon on loading the van.

"OK. I see we have a farewell party," Derrick said. "Careful how you use the term farewell party around these people," Rev. Carter whispered to Derrick.

"I'll keep that in mind. Simon, are we loaded?"

"He is now. You would have turned this van over before leaving the parking lot the way he had it loaded," Violet shouted.

"Do you mind if I say a prayer before these fine folks leave?" Rev. Carter asked loud enough not to give Derrick much say so. Derrick nervously gave him an OK wave. Rev. Carter cleared his throat, and in a loud, deep, authoritative tone started, "Our most exalted king on high, our humbling savior, our—"

"Good Lord," Karl replied.

Rev. Carter opened one eye, looking at Karl, "And our Good Lord!" He paused, then closed his eye. "Bless these fine people as they venture not only into a vacation but into a heavenly relationship with each other. Guide them safely back to us! Amen!"

Karl leaned over to the man he had been speaking with earlier. "He's on stage every Sunday." The old man just swallowed, not knowing what to say.

Before Derrick could say anything, Violet stepped in. "OK, people, here is how we are going to do it." She pointed at two of the new residents. "You two in the back." She looked at another lady, asking, "What do you weigh?"

Derrick stepped forward. "Let's just load how we are comfortable."

Violet gave him a direct stare, then threw her arms in the air. "It's your trip, Slim." She waved at the crowd, "Nice knowing you! It would have been nice for you to move in, but this jack-wagon is going to kill you!"

"Oh, for Pete's sake, just get in the damn van," Karl barked from the back.

Kat put her arm around Derrick. "You sure you don't need some extra help?"

He kissed her. "Good luck!"

Chapter 28

As the van exited left out of the gates and didn't tip over, a disappointed Violet huffed and marched to her ATV to drive back to her parking space. Kat stood under the awning like an elementary kid waving bye to her best friend, in this case her boyfriend. After a quick prayer asking for Jaqs to come down with a virus, she felt an arm slide across her shoulders; she looked to her left and Jack stood beside her watching the van disappear. "Well, kid, looks like it's just you and me." He smiled.

"Well, what do you think we can get into now that the cat is away?" she joked back. A smile formed across Jack's face. "You know I was just kidding," she quickly added.

"This place has everything but one essential key," Jack commented with some mystery.

Hesitantly replying, "What's that?" Kat asked.

"A bar."

"We have an area in the dining hall." She referred to a small, make-shift bar.

Jack raised an eyebrow and lifted the left side of his face. "Really?"

"Well, what do you have in mind?" "You know, a bar. Something classy."

Kat thought for a moment. "A few board members are coming Monday, and they always eat in the dining hall. Talk with them."

"I will, thanks. What is on your agenda?"

"Trying not to worry about Derrick off on a trip with Jaqs."

"Relax, what's the worst thing that could happen? Just remind her that employees are not allowed to date, and I'm sure she'll have a change of heart."

Kat smiled about Jack trying to make her feel better. "Thanks Jack."

"Unless it's just about sex and not a relationship," he replied, grinning. "It took a week and six old farts to convince Derrick to ask you out. You have nothing to worry about." He climbed back in his golf cart and drove toward the beach.

Kat knew she didn't have anything to worry about with Derrick—it was Jaqs that she worried the most about. She ducked back into Derrick's office and printed out an order form for the dining hall and then headed back out to the fitness center. With Jaqs on the trip, she had volunteered to sub her classes. Considering the number of people that went to Jaqs' classes, Kat hoped of people that went to Jaqs' classes, Kat hoped that she would be able to take the opportunity to advertise her art classes.

As she passed through the courtyard, Kat bumped into June, who was fixated on a rose bush. "They are beautiful," Kat said, looking over June's shoulder at the roses.

"Oh dear lord, Kat! You scared the bejeezus out of me."

"I'm sorry. Where you heading?" Kat asked. "Nowhere in particular, what about you?" "Fitness Center."

June wrapped her arm around Kat's and pulled herself close. "I'll go with you. Are you teaching now that big boobs is gone?"

"Big boobs?" Kat asked.

"Have you not seen the jugs that woman has? Why do you think most of her clients are men?"

A feeble man strolling by replied, "She got me exercising."

Laughing, the two of them continued their walk. "I agree with you, June, I don't think she's that beautiful."

"Oh! I didn't say that. She's a fox, and if I swung that way, I'd be chasing her too," June said, innocently looking at another rose brush.

"Thanks," Kat replied with a defeated expression, June stopped and looked over Kat's shoulder, "Oh, look. It's the tightly rounded little man from next door." Kat turned to see the resort manager walking their way.

"How can he walk in that suit? It's tighter than a mummy's wrap." June added.

Curious as to why the ladies were laughing, the manager spoke to Kat. "I was told that you are in charge this week."

Before she had time to answer, "How's it hanging Hank?" June blurted out.

"Hanging?" He asked.

"Your testicles? It's a slang that you young people use.

Haven't you heard it?" June said.

With a smug expression, "Yes, I've heard it." He directed his question back to Kat, "Well?"

"Oh, I don't have testicles." Kat couldn't help herself. She had heard Derrick complain many times about Hank and figured what could it hurt to pick on him.

"Very funny," he answered.

"Oh, Kat, that was funny," June replied with the giggles setting in.

"I'm sorry, what can I help you with?" Kat tried to keep a straight face, but with June snorting and huffing, trying to keep from laughing wasn't helping.

"We are hosting a party tomorrow tonight and would love—"

"What time does it start? We'd love to come," June interrupted him.

"Would love your residents not to interfere." He shot a stern glare at June.

"It's your property, you don't need my permission."

Straightening his suit jacket, "No, I don't need your permission, but there seems to be a discrepancy over who owns what part of the beach. I have tried to discuss this with the half-witted director here, but he seems to believe otherwise."

Now Kat wasn't laughing. "First, you know where the property boundaries lie, and secondly that half-witted director happens to be my boyfriend."

"Oh, I'm sorry. I would have picked you out to have someone more sophisticated to be partnered with."

"Like you," Kat answered in a sarcastic voice. "Perhaps someone of my demeanor, but I am not interested."

"Gay?" June asked. "I am not gay."

"But you wouldn't be interested in a hot girl like this?" June pointed at Kat with her hand.

"I didn't say—"

"So then you are gay? It's OK, you do remind me of Rock Hudson."

He tried to ignore June. "Tomorrow night is important to me, and I am professionally asking if you would keep the old kids home tomorrow tonight."

"You insult my boyfriend and now my friends here and you want me to help you?"

"Just stay away tomorrow tonight!" Hank turned and started back to the resort.

"You even have a sway like a gay man," June shouted, watching him walk. He turned and gave her a dirty look and tried to add more man to his stride.

Kat looked at June. "Whatcha say? Party tomorrow night?"

A smile formed on June's face. "I knew I liked you for a reason."

Chapter 29

Betty shook Karl from a deep sleep, "What's the matter? What time is it?" Karl sat up startled from his sleep.

"Nothing is the matter. It's 7:30 and time to get ready for church." Betty eased off the bed.

"OK, give me just a minute." Karl's head hit the pillow again, and after a second or two, he sat back up. "Church?" he yelled toward the bathroom. "Why in the hell are we going to church?"

Betty stuck her head out of the door. "I told Dianna we would come, and you can't be swearing on Sunday."

"Swearing on Sunday," he said under his breath. "So the reverend has his wife conning the other wives to church?"

"She didn't con me into going to church," Betty shouted back. Karl rubbed his head and tried to gain focus to find his house shoes, and Betty looked back out the door. "It's my job to con you into going. You can have chocolate cake at dinner."

Karl walked into the kitchen. "I can have chocolate cake at dinner," he sarcastically said to himself. "I'm not a damn child, you know," he yelled toward their bedroom. "Did you fix my coffee?" he continued.

"Yes, dear," she answered. "Or I should say, yes, my child." She giggled while putting on her makeup.

Karl walked out onto his balcony, a morning ritual that he enjoyed and didn't want to be interrupted. After blowing on his coffee mug, he set it on the table beside his chair, then walked back in for his paper. After separating and swearing at the coupons and advertising, he took the comics and important part of the paper back outside. Jack was sitting in his chair next to the railing and only eight inches from the Rutherfurds' balcony with his coffee sitting on his table, a mirror of each other.

"Karl," Jack addressed him, never looking up from his paper.

"Goslin," Karl answered. And for the next 20 minutes, they sat quietly reading the paper and drinking their coffees until Betty broke the silence.

"Karl, we are going to be late if you don't get ready. Good morning, Jack," she said.

"Good morning." Jack's eyes never left the paper. "Where are you going?"

"She wants to go to church." "Church!" Jack looked over.

"She's bribing me like a little kid, says I can have a piece of chocolate cake if I go. Can you believe that? I'm a grown man!"

"How big is the piece of cake?" Jack asked.

"I don't know; it's that seven-layer cake they make at the dining hall."

"The old diabetes-on-a-plate cake," Jack responded.

Karl shook his head. "It does sound good." He shot up from his chair. "Then it's settled. You're going with us!"

"Settled? What was there to settle?"

"See you in 10 minutes." Karl said, ducking back inside before Jack could answer.

"I'm not part of your marriage!" He yelled at the glass door, then he looked out toward the gulf. "Or am I?" He shook his head.

A few minutes later, Jack heard a knock on the door, and opening it he found Betty. "Oh, Jack, I am so happy you have decided to go to church with us."

Jack looked over Betty at Karl smiling in the hallway. "Me too," he answered with a smirk.

On the way to church, Betty walked tall and proud that she had not only accomplished getting her husband to church, but his friend too. As they approached the chapel, Rev. Carter and Dianna were out front greeting people with the double doors open. "They look like they're running for office," Karl muttered.

"Well, my oh my! Hell did freeze over!" Rev. Carter shouted out at the sight of Karl and Jack joining Betty.

"Only if the Dallas Cowboys lose today," Betty laughed, switching hands with her ice tea to shake hands. "You know she'll leave if you go too long past kickoff," Karl warned.

"Oh, I'm a fan too. God's team. We'll be done just before kickoff," Rev. Carter belted out, then lowered his voice. "Kickoff is at 3 today, so I can go longer." He grinned at Karl.

"Are you going to turn any water to wine today?" Jack firmly shook the reverend's hand.

"I'll see what I can do."

"Karl and Jack! At my service, today is going to be the Lord's Day," Rev. Carter joyfully shouted from the door, causing everyone inside to look back.

"Don't get too excited; I'm only here for the chocolate cake," Karl replied and pushed his way inside.

"Chocolate?" Rev. Carter looked at Jack.

"He wasn't referring to you; he's talking about lunch." Jack pushed in with Karl, leaving the reverend questioning the cake remark.

After 30 minutes of pounding on the pulpit and sounding more like a political candidate than a preacher, Karl starting watching the time. At 10 a.m., the time service was supposed to end, the reverend was still going strong. Karl leaned over to Betty and pointed at his watch. Betty pushed his hand back and patted him on the leg. Three minutes later, Karl leaned back over, saying in a loud whisper, "Jack and I are leaving. Al Sharpton up there is going to make me miss my cake!"

"It will be over in a few," she whispered back. A couple in front of Karl stood up and left, and Betty firmly grabbed Karl's leg to keep him from slipping out with them.

Karl looked over at Jack, who was calmly sitting in the pew. "How can you sit so patiently?" he asked.

Jack took out his ear bud. "What?" "You're listening to the radio?"

"A western story. Kat showed me how to download books." Jack placed the ear piece back in his ear.

Finally, after going over by 15 minutes and losing over half his congregation, Rev. Carter ended the service. As Betty and the other wives walked up front to shake hands with Rev. Carter Karl, Jack, and what men were left quickly exited and headed toward the dining hall. A line met them in the hallway, and after waiting, Karl finally got in front of the food. He pointed at the pork chop, three sides, and a roll. After pushing the couple in front of him, he made it to the desert rack. It was layered with pies, cookies, pudding, and an empty spot for their famous seven-layer cake.

"Well, son of a" The entire room fell into silence looking at one mad and upset Alabamian.

Chapter 30

With one day down on the orientation trip, Derrick flung his luggage on the bed and took out his shower kit for a quick shower before he had to be back downstairs for supper. After turning on the hot water and steaming up the bathroom, he set his cell phone on the dresser and disappeared into the steam. Stepping into the shower, he didn't hear the light knock at his door, and after a second knock the doorknob slowly turned, and since he had forgotten to lock his door in the turn-of-the-century hotel, Jaqs walked in.

Back at CBC, Kat had experienced a pretty simple day, with the exception of an angry man in the dining hall over a chocolate cake, but after asking the kitchen to bake another cake, things had settled down. She picked up her cell phone and looked at the time. "Derrick should be checked in by now," she said to herself, dialing his number.

On the third ring, she heard an answer, just not what she expected. "Hello," the voice answered. Kat froze for a second, thinking she had dialed the wrong number.

"Hello?" Kat asked.

"Can I help you?" the voice on the other end asked. "Who is this?"

"I'm sorry, this is Jaqueline Silva, Derrick's assistant. Who am I speaking with?" She knew.

"You're not his assistant! Put Derrick on the phone!" Kat ordered.

"Oh, Kat! I wouldn't have answered if I knew it was you." She paused and made her way closer to the bathroom so Kat could hear the shower in the background. "Derrick is in the shower. Maybe I should have him call you back and explain."

In disbelief, Kat looked at her cell phone. "Don't bother!" Kat hung up in shock and fell in the desk chair. "Surely I am imaging this?" She dialed Simon's phone and didn't give him any time to answer when he picked up. "Simon, go to Derrick's room and see if Jaqs is there!"

"What?"

"Just go!"

He rolled off his bed. "OK, hang on." Walking into the hall, he ran into Jaqs leaving Derrick's room.

"Oh, hey Simon," Jaqs looked surprised and placed her index finger over her lips, "Can we stay quiet about this?" And then slipped into her room across the hall.

Simon stood in the hallway holding his cell phone, not sure what he was witnessing. "Um, yeah?" he said into his phone.

"Jaqs is in Derrick's room?" Kat asked.

"She was. She just went back to her room across the hall."

"Her room is across the hall from Derrick's?" "Yes."

Kat shook her head in disbelief. "OK," she said, then hung up. "I can't believe I'm this gullible."

Unaware of everything that had just happened, Derrick dried off and got dressed to get to the restaurant before anyone else. On his way down the stairs, he reached in his back pocket for his phone and realized he had left it in his room. As he made his way into the elegantly laid out restaurant, he saw that two of the people on his trip were already there, so going back after his phone wasn't an option. "Did you folks find everything in your rooms OK?" he asked, striking up a conversation and thinking that Kat was probably trying to call or text him to check in.

Kat calling or texting him was the last thing that was going to happen, but she wasn't going to let others know what was going on. She had wanted to prove that she could run CBC, and the last thing she wanted people to know was the drama that was unfolding. Gathering the files and budget reports the director had prepared, she placed them in front of each seat in the board room along with a bottle of water.

"Kat?" A voice called her from the doorway.

She looked back to see one of the assistants. "Hey, what are you doing here on Sunday?" She wiped her eyes, hoping they didn't look red.

"I forgot a few things. There are two policemen here looking for you."

"For goodness gracious, who's done what?" She rolled her eyes and followed the young girl out into the offices.

"Mrs. Rose?" one of the officers asked.

"Ms. But call me Kat. What can I do for you?"

"The manager from next door called and wanted to file a complaint about a hostile conversation you had with him. Were you hostile with him?"

She stood silent for a moment, thinking of the guts he had for calling in a lie. "I wasn't, but wait until the next time I see him."

The other officer laughed, causing the first one to give him a funny look. "He also said he was hosting a party for his guests this evening and wanted to hire off-duty officers to make sure they weren't disturbed. I don't think that is necessary, but I do know you guys have a dispute over property boundaries."

"He's constantly using our property, and it upsets the residents here. Anything that happens to that weasel and his party, well, he deserves it. If he is on our property, I can't promise anything."

"Please do what you can. I don't want that weasel . . . manager to have any true complaints on you guys," the officer said with a smile.

"I will. Thank you." She followed them outside, where they bumped into Violet. Her eyes grew twice their size, and they could have seen her heart pumping if they had looked closer.

"Ma'am," one of the officers said to her. Before she could answer them, the officer who had spoken received a call about a biker gang at the liquor store causing problems. He looked at his partner, saying, "We better go."

"What was that about?" Violet asked Kat.

"The manager next door called in a complaint about me and their party tonight."

"Oh, thank God."

Kat looked at her funny. "You got something going on I should know about?" she said with a smile.

"Nope. Have a good day," Violet said, and quickly scurried off.

The unusual conversation she had with the officers and Violet took her mind off Derrick for only a short moment. As she walked toward the parking lot, a knot formed in her stomach as the realization of Derrick cheating on her came to light. She did her best to fight off the tears and looked around—it seemed that Jack always had a way of showing up during her tough times. But this time he wasn't in sight, so she shut her door and cranked the engine, and before her vehicle could warm up, her shirt became drenched in tears.

Chapter 31

Violet burst in her door to find Jack, Karl, Betty, June, and in disbelief, the reverend. Violet pointed at Rev. Carter and looked at Jack, demanding, "Can he be trusted?"

"He's a man of the cloth," Jack answered.

She raised up with a smug look. "That doesn't give him an instant card of trust." Rev. Carter laughed, but stopped when Violet looked at him. "How do we know you won't turn us in or try to stop us from going too far?"

"I stole cars in my youth, you don't think—"

Violet interrupted him before he could explain any more. "OK! He'll do." She grabbed a bottle of wine and an arm full of mugs.

"Mugs and wine?" Rev. Carter asked. "Your point?"

"No point."

"Jack." Violet took a swig from the bottle, "I overheard on a policeman's radio that a biker gang was causing problems at the liquor store. Do you think we could use them tonight?"

Jack nodded. "I believe we can, I'm on it." He turned up his mug of wine and headed out the door before anyone could say anything.

Rev. Carter watched him disappear out the door, then looked back at Violet, thinking, Biker gang? Maybe I am over my head.

"Rutherfurd, did you get them?" Violet asked like a five-star general would in a war room conversation.

A smile formed across his face. "Yep."

"Good, let me change and we'll wait on Jack, then head over."

Rev. Carter leaned over to Karl. "What did you get?" Karl cut his eyes at the reverend. "TNT."

It took Rev. Carter a minute for it to register; then he leaned back to Karl, asking, "Seriously?"

"You wanted in, too late now." Karl sipped on a glass of ice tea Betty had fixed him, then tilted it toward Rev. Carter. "Whiskey?"

The reverend started a silent prayer. "What are we doing with dynamite?" he asked, getting nervous, then saw a snicker come from Karl. "What are we really doing?" he asked louder.

Karl started laughing. "You should have seen your face. TNT and whiskey."

"Oh, ha-ha! This is a racist thing, uh?" Karl stopped laughing. "Racist?"

"Was my expression like that?" He pointed at Karl's face smiling.

Violet came back out to find June and Betty talking over a blouse and Karl and the reverend laughing over ice tea and wine. Jack had started toward the liquor store when he spotted the bikers coming down toward him, and with a flash of his golf cart lights and an arm waving them down, they pulled over to see what the old man wanted. And with a few Benjamin's flashed, he had their attention. The other five at the apartment waited impatiently for the call from Jack to say what he was planning.

A text came to Violet's phone: "Give our beloved biker gang 15 minutes to attend the party, and you should be in the clear for at least a half hour."

"I'm not sure what Jack is planning, but we have 30 minutes to disburse the weapon in Hank's office," Violet said.

"What weapon?" Rev. Carter shouted.

Karl picked up his jacket with a tube under it. "Three hundred crickets!" he said as he proudly held up the tube of crickets.

They headed toward the resort, hearing a dozen Harley Davidsons pull in their parking lot at the beach. And as stealthily as an elderly couple from Alabama, two sisters from Arkansas, and a black preacher from the hood could be, they made their way across the property boundary and onto the resort. Karl, Rev. Carter, and Violet crouched over and lightly ran to the first building, while Betty and June walked behind them laughing and gossiping about something they had heard earlier.

"Will you two get down!?!" Karl waved at them.

"Oh, relax. Those cameras picked you up 100 feet back there," June said, pointing at two security cameras mounted on the corner of the building.

"We've only gone 100 feet?" Rev. Carter panted. "And why is it taking five of us to let 300 crickets go?"

"They're vicious little critters!" Violet replied. Rev. Carter wasn't sure if she was serious or not. Karl pulled on the first door he came to and held it open for the other four, and after he looked both ways, he closed the door as the fearsome five disappeared in the resort to emancipate their biological weapons.

After thirty minutes of running from hallway to hallway looking for the manager's office, they finally made it to a foyer with five doors, one reading "Resort Manager." "Thank God, I don't work that much in Jaqs' class," Betty said, sitting down to catch her breath.

Jack slipped into the office with the tube of crickets and opened the top, shaking the container wildly with crickets flying all over the office. He opened the door and gave everyone the thumbs up. "Let's get out of here!" Violet said and headed out, followed by the others. Once they reached the outdoors, the five of them broke into a run toward the same path they came over. And while running, they heard the dozen Harleys roaring down the street, meaning their diversion was over.

Karl ran behind the reverend and the two sisters, and once he reached the end of the white fence that separated the two properties, he reached back to help Betty. Without looking, he said, "Give me your hand," but got no response. Looking back, he called out, "Betty?" He glanced at the others, thinking maybe she was in front of him, but only three of the crew was in front.

He walked back down the alley they had run up to see if he could see her, finding nothing. Out of breath and on wobbly legs, he jogged back, whispering, "Betty?" His eyes searched back and forth on the back alley, and he was almost to the door they had run out when he saw something out of the ordinary. "Betty?" he said louder, looking at a shadow of something lying near the fence.

He stepped closer and the color of her blouse caught his sight. "Betty!" He picked up his trot. "Oh, dear God, Betty?" He made it to her side, where she was lying on her left side and unresponsive. Like a small child not knowing what to do, he got on his knees beside her, shaking her, "Honey, wake up. Open your eyes." Panic overwhelmed his body.

Karl fell to a sitting position, pulling Betty into his lap. "Betty, wake up." His voice grew louder. Her left arm fell limp to the pavement and her head fell back, and Karl screamed, "Help, somebody help us!" Tears blurred his vision, and the world stopped. After fifty-eight years, Karl's greatest fear was coming true, a fear of Betty leaving him.

Chapter 32

Kat was the first to the hospital, finding Karl in the waiting room of the ER sitting by himself slumped over with his face in his hands. Feeling the warm hand of Kat resting on his shoulder, he looked up at her, not able to speak. Kat rubbed his back. "How is she?"

Without speaking, Karl shrugged his shoulders, insinuating he wasn't sure. "Let me check." Kat set her purse down and walked to the window with a nurse sitting behind it.

Sliding open the window, the nurse asked if she could help Kat. "I am checking on Betty Rutherfurd."

"One second." The nurse held up her index finger and walked to the back.

Moments later, another nurse opened the door leading to the back. "Hi, you are asking about Mrs. Rutherfurd?"

"Yes, how is she?"

"May I ask your relationship with her?"

"I am the acting director at CBC," Kat answered.

The nurse waved her to step in the doors. "Come back for a second." She led Kat to the nurse's station, where three other nurses were busy going over charts and entering reports on their computer. "This is the director of CBC." The nurse spoke to a doctor reading over a file folder.

He looked at her over his glasses, "I assume you are here about Mrs. Rutherfurd."

"I am."

He walked around the nurse station, giving Kat an uneasy feeling with the news he was about to deliver. "She is doing fine," he replied. Kat took a large breath of air in relief. "We are running tests, but everything points to a heart attack. She is lucky that the paramedics were nearby. We will probably keep her a few days and run a few other tests."

"Can her husband see her?" "Of course."

Kat turned and walked to the door, opened it and waved at Karl to come back. "Betty is doing great," she told him. "Why don't you go see her?" Kat pointed toward the nurse's station to find out what room she was in.

"Right this way, Mr. Rutherfurd." A young nurse took Karl by the hand and led him to a room with a partially closed curtain. Kat could hear both Karl and Betty talking, but couldn't make out what was said.

"For the most part, she seems to be very healthy, but these tests will be able to tell us everything we need to know," the doctor told Kat.

The nurse at the window returned. "There is an older gentleman here asking for you. I can only allow two people back at a time." She spoke to Karl.

"I'll see who it is," Kat replied, following the nurse back to the front.

Jack stood in the middle of the waiting room, holding his hat with a set of nervous hands. Kat smiled as she walked out, giving him some relief. "She is doing fine."

"Thank God! We'd have to move Karl to the psych department if something happened to her," he replied. Kat wasn't sure if he was joking or not. "Can I go back?" He pointed with his hat.

Kat looked at the nurse, who smiled and waved him back. Watching them disappear through the doors, she reached for her cell phone and paused, knowing she should call Derrick first, but he was the last person she wanted to talk to. She thumbed through her contacts and pulled up the director's number. Pushing the button, she tried to rehearse what she was going to say.

"Good evening, Kat," the director answered.

"Sorry to bother you, but Betty Rutherfurd was rushed to the hospital this evening with heart troubles. She is doing fine now, we are at the hospital."

"Yes, I have already heard." Kat paused, wondering how she learned about the incident so quickly. "Hank from next door called me," the director continued.

"Hank?"

"The manager next door."

"Yes, I know who he is, but why did he call you?"

"Well, it was on his property, and something about a biker gang crashing his party. I don't know, he gets worked up pretty easy."

Not having a clue about what the biker gang had anything to do with Betty's heart attack, Kat went back to her original intent. "I wanted to let you know."

"What did Derrick say?" the director asked. "I haven't called him yet."

"He needs to be the first one you call from now on," she answered.

"He's the last one I want to talk to," she replied before she realized what she was saying.

"If you and Derrick are having problems, you better not let it interfere with your duties as acting director. I asked for you to take the role because you have such a great history at CBC. Don't screw that up with a scrabble with your boyfriend." The director's voice grew.

Kat finished her conversation with the director, but then, still not wanting to talk to Derrick, she texted him everything, adding that she didn't want to speak with him and had everything handled. As she was finishing her message, she saw Karl and Jack walk out of the corridor and make their way to the back of the waiting room. Looking at her phone, she started to check on them, but seeing Karl upset, she stopped, knowing Jack was there for him.

Karl had asked Jack to step out with him, not wanting to worry or upset Betty. Jack, unaware of why Karl asked him to step outside, turned to him in the waiting room to witness Karl break down, sobbing uncontrollably. Jack wasn't sure what to do, not ever having to console someone, so on a gamble he put his arm around the man, who in turned bear hugged him. Jack looked at Kat, confused on what to do, so he patted Karl on the back, whispering something in his ear that Kat couldn't hear.

After a long five minutes, Karl gathered himself, and without words, nodded to Jack in thanks and for that guy code not to tell anyone that he was crying. Jack had to wipe his eyes to tell Karl everything was going to be all right, his tears partially for Karl and for himself not having someone in his life the way Karl did. "Go back and be with Betty. I'll be right here," Jack said with a smile at his best friend.

Chapter 33

Derrick sat on the edge of his bed before breakfast, his cell phone glued to his ear with the director on the other end giving him the riot act for causing drama at CBC. One of the many qualities that Derrick posed was not laying the blame on others, whether right or wrong, so he remained quiet on the phone. It was a trait that the director knew all too well, but with him essentially in charge, it fell on his shoulders. "CBC has a policy about dating employees to avoid distractions like this, and if Kat wasn't favorite with the board she'd be fired."

"But she—" Derrick started against his character to defend Kat.

"I know," the director interrupted him. "Perhaps you should explain the rules to Jaqs better so she understands I have no problem firing her. Now, I am packing up things here and heading back to CBC, so I should be there tomorrow."

"Does Kat know you're coming back?"

"I'll let her know this morning. Are you having a good trip?"

"Yes."

"OK, I need to go put an end to this revenge on the resort before someone dies. I'll see you when you get back." She hung up without giving Derrick a chance to say goodbye.

He set on the bed looking at his cell phone, wanting to talk to Kat, but she hadn't answered the prior six calls. Frustrated, he tossed his phone toward his bag in the corner and stood in front of the dresser pouring another cup of coffee from the small, shoddy coffee maker. A light knock came from his door, and without looking out the peep hole, he pulled open the door to see Jaqs standing in the doorway.

Not the person he needed to see first thing this morning. "Can I help you?" he grunted.

"Did we wake up on the wrong side of the bed?" Jaqs asked.

"I think you know why I am upset."

"Let me make it up to you." She squeezed between the doorjamb and his body.

Derrick never left the doorway. "You need to leave!" "Nobody is up yet. I promised to be quiet." She signaled him over with her index finger and slowly sat on the bed.

"First of all, this is a senior trip. Everyone has been up since 5 a.m. taking their meds, drinking coffee, and complaining to each other. Second, it is clear that you didn't read the employee handbook about employees not allowed to be involved with each other romantically!"

"Rules, smules! They're created to break."

"Either leave or pack your bags and head back to Florida—am I clear!" Derrick exclaimed.

Jaqs stood up and pushed her way past Derrick. "There's more fish in the sea," she replied, but when she looked back, Derrick had already closed his door.

On her way to work, Kat swung by the hospital to check in on Betty and to retrieve Jack, who had moved from one waiting room to another. Kat walked in to find Jack slouched in a chair with his fedora hat pulled over his eyes and his arms crossed in front of him. She gently nudged him. "I'm still breathing," he replied without looking up.

"Why don't you ride back with me to CBC," Kat said in a soft voice.

Jack pulled his hat back. "I thought you were the young nurse who kept coming by to make sure I was still alive." He stretched his arms over his head. "Derrick is a lucky man."

"Come on." She ignored the comment. After they checked in on Betty and Karl, they walked down to her vehicle and headed back to CBC. Traffic was light, and the ride back was silent and quick. "Do you want me to drop you off at the Towers?"

"Nah, I'm heading to the dining hall." He didn't wait for Kat and walked toward the dining hall with two things in mind, coffee and food. He could barely get in the door before half a dozen people surrounded him with a million questions about Betty. He started to tell everyone that she was dead, thinking that would buy him enough of time to get his coffee and breakfast, but instead muscled his way to the buffet line.

Picking up his tray, he scanned the tables for someone to sit with. Violet and June were sitting by the window arguing over their day. "Pull up a chair, Goslin!" Violet shouted loud enough for the people in the resort next door to hear.

"How's Betty?" June asked in a softer voice. "She's good."

"Rutherfurd?" Violet asked.

"He's good too." Jake took a sip from his cup and noticed the same flock of people asking the same questions swarmed Kat as she entered the doors. Kat managed to fend off the people, and when Jack pulled back the empty chair at their table, she sat her tray down.

"Good morning, ladies," she greeted them.

June punched Jack. "She called you a lady," she laughed.

"Actually, I've already said good morning to him." "Yep, nudged me to wake up. Something I could get used to." He grinned.

"Oh, something we should know and hide from Derrick?" Violet laughed.

"I picked him up at the hospital." Kat rolled her eyes. "How's Derrick doing on the trip?" June changed the subject.

Violet wiped her mouth with the back of her hand. "Shoot! You are a very trustworthy gal to allow him to go with that half-dressed Brazilian chick. If I swung both ways, I'd be after her."

"Please, you haven't swung in 40 years," June rolled her eyes. "Ignore her—Derrick is a fine man and wouldn't do anything to jeopardize your relationship."

If you only knew, Kat thought as her phone buzzed with a text from the director. Reading it, she wasn't sure what to process with the director returning early from her trip. She looked up to see Violet elbow Jack and point at two men dressed in suits standing in the doorway looking around the tables.

Kat looked back. "Who are they?" she said out loud and started to go ask.

"Keep your seat. They're looking for me," Jack said, setting his napkin in his chair and going to greet the mysterious men. After a few minutes of conversation with the three ladies watching him, he waved over Violet, leaving June and Kat at the table.

"June, do you know them?" Kat asked, seeing June had gone back to eating.

"Nope."

"Are you curious?" "Nope."

Kat watched Violet, Jack, and the two men disappear out the door and head back to the Towers.

Chapter 34

The morning seemed pretty quiet, with the exception of Violet zooming around in her ATV wearing her white helmet and scarf flapping in the wind. Kat cleaned out her belongings from the director's office in preparation for her return. She was setting the new agenda for the board meeting in front of each chair when she heard the ladies in the office talk about lunch. She walked in the office to join their conversation when the two mysterious men in suits passed by the door heading to the parking lot. She dashed out the door to catch them and find out what they were doing when Violet slid to a stop between her and the two men. "How's Betty doing?" she asked pulling her helmet off.

Kat craned over the ATV to see where the men had gone. "She is doing fine. They will return tomorrow morning. Who are those men that you and Jake were talking to?" She pointed to the men.

Violet looked back, then at Kat. "They're friends of Jack. Business partners."

"I thought Jack was retired." She looked at Violet. "That's what he claims, but Jack has always got something going on." She smashed her helmet back down on her head.

"Does it have something to do with why Jack wants to talk to the board today?" Kat asked over the engine of Violet's ATV.

Violet said something, but with the engine noise and the muffled voice from her helmet, Kat couldn't make out her answer, and before she had a chance to ask again, Violet spun the back tires and jetted toward the bridge leading to the beach. An elderly couple jumped out of her way, something the residents were getting used to.

Determined to find out who the men were and Jack's true agenda, Kat headed to the dining hall. After looking at her watch, she knew he'd be at lunch. Walking in the doors, she met the same group of people from this morning surrounding her and asking the same questions about Betty. She wondered if they even remembered the answers from this morning.

Surveying the tables again, she spotted Jack sitting with Sylvia and a few of her friends. "You are quite the celebrity around here," Jack smiled, pointing at the ladies that had followed her to the table.

"Ladies, if you don't mind, I need to talk to Jack," she politely said.

"We don't mind," one of the ladies answered, not moving.

Another lady grabbed her by the arm. "She means leave them alone," and pulled her back to their table.

"We can make room if you'd like to join us?" Sylvia replied.

"No, thank you, Jack, can I speak with you for a moment?" She motioned to an empty table. Jack set his napkin in his chair and followed Kat to the table. "Who were those men that you met with this morning?"

"Consultants," he answered. "For?"

"Business. What's with the questions? Are you worried about something?" Jack picked up on her nervous twitch. "You wanted to meet with the board today and then these mysterious men showed up. I just didn't want to be blindsided with something crazy today with the director coming back."

"Why is the director cutting her vacation short?" "It's a long story."

Jack pulled back a chair and took a seat. "That's all I have is time. What's the story?"

For the next 20 minutes, Kat poured out everything to Jack, a person that had always been on her side. Toward the end of her story, she fought the tears back, and with her voice cracking Jack stepped in. "I stand by judgement. I bet there is more to the story; Derrick sure does love you, and I know he wouldn't do anything to jeopardize that."

"My heart wants to believe that, but my head is being more rational. She was in his room with the shower running in the background."

"Here's my advice: With the director coming back, just go back to your normal every day, and when Derrick gets back, you guys will have more time together."

"I don't want to compete with her. She is very popular here," Kat answered.

"Skimpy clothes, flirtation, and a healthy set of boobs will do that," Jack answered.

"Jack!"

"Don't let insecurities get in the way of your relationship with Derrick," Jack replied. It was something that Kat denied, but hearing Jack say it made it come to life with her. She sat back in her chair thinking about the comment. "As far as the board. I am just asking if we can open a community bar here. Either build something or remodel. That's it."

"I'm sorry. I didn't mean to interrupt your lunch with your girlfriend." Kat stood up.

"Sylvia? She's just a friend."

"That's what they all say," Kat said. "I'll see you in an hour at the board meeting."

Within the hour after Jack managed to scarf down his lunch, he went back to his apartment to collect a file folder and head to the meeting. When he walked in, the members were already sitting talking with the director, who still had her brief case hanging from her shoulder. They greeted Jack and had him sit at the head of the conference table to pitch his idea about a bar. When the predictable early grumbling about the finances of the proposed bar arose, Jack interjected that he would pay for the construction or remodeling. As the members were now buying into the idea, Kat slipped out to change for her class that she was subbing for Jaqs.

Standing in front of a mirror changing, Kat looked at the shirt she was wearing and shaking her head. If Jaqs can teach wearing what she is comfortable with, then so can I! She pulled off the shirt, leaving a modest sports bra revealed, and headed out.

"Are you guys ready?" She greeted the class that was now mostly women.

"Wow! Look at you, Kat," one lady replied, then patted Kat's stomach, "You're all muscle."

An elderly man in the back of the room responded, "Let me check!"

"No, that's OK." Kat started to question her decision, but when the back door opened and half a dozen men walked in, she decided to go with it. "OK, everyone grab a mat and let's stretch." Two more men entered the building, and Kat smiled, "You know, I also teach art here."

"Like that? Sign me up," one of the men yelled from the back.

Chapter 35

Sitting on his balcony in a state of depression, Jack toked on a cigar, looking at the empty chair that Karl usually sat in. While he contemplated whether to open a bottle of bourbon, a loud and forceful knock came from his door. Hesitant to open, he heard the culprit, Violet. "Open up, Goslin!" she yelled loud enough to wake everyone in the Tower Apartments.

"Hold your horses," Jack said, turning the deadbolt. Violet shoved her way through the door. "Thank goodness I was dressed," Jack said, surprised at her presentence.

"Well, it's not like I haven't seen one before. With Rutherfurd gone, I figured you could use some company!" She held up a bottle of her Merlot.

"Come on back." He waved her to the balcony, grabbing two glasses on his way back out.

Violet handed him the bottle, then leaned over the balcony, "Three flights sure makes a difference."

"Difference?"

"We don't get this view from the second floor." She looked up at the next two stories, "Anyone above you?"

"Not above the Rutherfurds. You and June should move up there." Jack chuckled inside, thinking about the fit Karl would throw if Violet lived above him.

"Might do that."

Jack sat in his chair, opened the drawer from the table that separated his chair from Karl's, and took out a bottle opener. After pulling the cork, he poured a glass for both of them.

"Thank you," Violet replied, taking a big swig, then wiping her mouth with the back of her hand. "You and Westheimer dating?"

Jack almost spit his wine out. "Sylvia? Nah, just friends."

"Yea, I need me one of those type of friends. Most of the men around here don't seem interested." She leaned over the balcony and spit a red loogie into the wind.

Jack cringed. "I can't imagine why."

"Right!" She looked at him, then sat in Karl's chair. "I feel bad for Putts."

"Karl." Jack corrected her.

Not catching the hint, Violet agreed, "Yes, Karl. What could I do for him?" She leaned back, rocking back and forth.

"He's a simple man. Hard to do something for people like that."

"Yep. Say, you have the number for the man that customized your golf cart?" She changed the subject, or

Jack thought she had. He pulled out his cell phone and showed her the number. Kat had still been working with Jack on teaching him his cell phone, and at one point she had showed him how to share numbers through texting and air-dropping. After calling 911 four times in a row, though, Jack decided he'd just write the number down the old fashioned way.

"You looking for some work on your ATV?" he asked. "Something like that," she answered, then downed her glass of wine. "Thanks for the company." She climbed to her feet.

"Company? You haven't been here five minutes," Jack looked at her.

"Just thought of something I forgot. Enjoy the wine, and thanks for putting me on those two wine buyers."

"Keep that under wraps," Jack answered. "Without a liquor license, you and I are bona fide bootleggers."

Violet grinned real big. "Feels good to be a rebel, doesn't it?"

"Not if we get caught," Jack emphasized. Violet walked out laughing at his remark, making him nervous that her blabbing would get them caught.

The elevator doors weren't closed before Violet had dialed the number that Jack had given her and asked, "Hey, is this the man that customized Jack Goslin's golf cart?"

"It is, what can I do for you?" The man replied.

"It's not me, but a friend of mine. His wife is in the hospital, and I want to do something nice for him. Can you come pick up a golf cart this evening?"

"We are closing pretty soon, what about tomorrow?"

"Not going to work. It has to be tonight, and I don't care what it costs. I'm paying cash."

"We'll be there in five minutes."

"Meet me at the golf cart parking." She hung up the phone and proudly stepped off the elevator to cut loose Karl's cart.

Violet opened her toolbox and took out the bolt cutters she kept, but before she could cut the lock, a voice startled her. "Am I interrupting a crime in progress?" Hank the resort manager said, standing in the shadows.

"You do realize I'm carrying the same pistol I shot your ATV tires with," she reminded him.

He took a big gulp and stepped into the light. "I would like to call peace for the time being."

"Why? Tired of losing?"

"Let's just say I'm interested in a certain wine." He lifted his left eyebrow.

Violet knew he was aware of her operation and thought about denying it, but wanted to hear him out. "What about it?"

"I'd like to place an order for ten cases. If you have that much," he taunted.

"When?"

"Tonight, if possible."

A flatbed truck pulled into the parking lot. "Tell you what. Hold that lock." She pointed to Karl's golf cart locked to a post. "Help me load the cart, and we'll go get your wine. Deal?"

Without answering, Hank bent over and picked up the lock for Violet to cut it, but instead a flash of light blinded him. Once he was able to get his sight back, he saw Violet holding her phone and taking his picture. "There, a picture of you stealing Karl's cart should keep you and I on the up and up," she grinned.

"I assure you my intentions are to make sure my guests are receiving the finest, and word on the street your wine is the best." He continued to hold the lock, gaining Violet's trust. She cut the lock and turned to speak with the man in the truck.

"What all are you wanting on the cart?" the man asked.

"The works!" she smiled.

"Jack's was the first golf cart we customized." He walked around the cart, "Stripes?"

"Yep." Violet answered liking the idea, then adding, "Stereo and speakers."

"Fifteen's?" The man asked.

"Sure." Violet didn't have a clue what fifteen's meant. "Bigger tires with chrome wheels, the one's that keep spinning when you stop. And! Put some of those neon lights underneath so he can see them at night." She backed up and looked at it again, "Make it faster!"

"OK, it's going to take a good day. How about we bring it back day after tomorrow?" The man asked.

"Sounds good." Violet looked at Hank. "Help us push it up on the truck."

Hank took off his suit jacket and laid it across a nearby bush and got behind the cart to push, and another light flashed in his eyes.

"Can't never be too sure," Violet grinned, taking another picture of Hank stealing Karl's golf cart.

Chapter 36

Karl walked beside Betty, who was being pushed in a wheel chair to the front door, where Kat was waiting for them. With little sleep, Karl's patience was pushed to the limits, and after an argument over whether he could take home a half dozen Jell-O cups, he was ready leave. "Good morning! You sure look beautiful," Kat greeted them.

"We would have been released an hour ago, but she insisted on fixing her hair. I don't know why—it's just a damn hospital!" Karl grumbled.

"You never know who you are going to run into." Kat smiled at Betty.

"Right. I try to explain to him, but he never understands." Betty stood and whispered to Kat, "It's not just a guy thing, it's a Karl thing." Kat covered her giggle. "Is that everything?" The young orderly asked, closing the backdoor for Betty.

"You can walk your ass in there and get me 6 Jell-O's!" Karl barked. The orderly's eyes grew, not knowing the fuss Karl had given earlier.

"No, we are good." Kat turned to Karl, "We can stop and get you Jell-O on the way home."

"It ain't the same," he pouted, slamming his door.

After a quiet ride back to CBC, Kat pulled to the front door of the Towers and popped her trunk for Betty's bags. The elevator doors opened and June and Violet stepped off. June threw her arms around Betty, and Karl forced his way past them and onto the elevator. "I'm so happy you're home! Do you want us to save you a seat at the breakfast table?" June said.

"Y'all come on! Can't keep the elevator waiting," Karl said.

Violet stared him down. "Putts," she nodded to him. "Redneck," Karl answered.

Betty walked on the elevator. "No, I better rest. But save us seats for lunch."

"Kat, can we talk with you?" Violet asked as Karl pushed the fifth floor button over and over.

"Sure, I'm here all day."

The doors started to close. "We want to move to the apartment above Karl and Betty." Violet replied.

Karl's eyes grew three times their size just as the elevator door shut, "Like hell—"

It was the longest five flights that Kat had ever ridden on an elevator, and Kat wasn't sure that Karl ever took a breath while he went through an extensive list of why the Stevens sisters couldn't move above them. Slowly and trying to be unnoticed, she pushed the fifth floor button just to make sure it was going to stop. As the doors opened, Karl stepped off, still mad as a wet hen. Betty smiled at Kat, commenting that "You get used to it."

Jack stood in his doorway to greet them. "I take it Violet asked about moving on the sixth floor." Jack thumbed toward Karl.

Karl stopped and looked at him. "Did you get my paper this morning?"

Jack pulled it out from behind him, "Didn't even open it." Karl snatched it from him, then headed into his apartment.

"He's heading to the library," Betty smiled and thanked Jack. Kat followed her into their apartment, set down her bags, and made sure she was OK before leaving. Karl fought through the paper trying not to get more upset, but every five minutes he'd holler out something about dumb asses in the world. The only comfort Betty got out of his outburst was that she knew he was still breathing.

Karl heard the doorbell, then Betty talking, then silence. He looked at the bathroom door as he heard the doorbell again, Betty talking, then silence. This went on for 15 minutes until he couldn't handle the curiosity and walked out to find the island in the kitchen was covered with casseroles and a few balloons.

"What's this?" He asked.

"People have been coming by bringing food," she said as the doorbell rang again. Opening the door Rev.

Carter and Dianna said welcome home holding another casserole.

Walking in Karl greeted them, "She didn't die!" "Well, of course not, we just wanted to bring over a welcome home gift," Dianna smiled. "Casserole is for dead people!" Karl argued.

Waving his hand in front of his nose, Rev. Carter asked, "Speaking of dead, what happened in here?"

Karl smiled real big. "Me." He walked to the door and opened it, "And since you can't handle it, thanks for coming."

Betty pushed the door closed, "He's kidding." She shot him a tired look.

"Betty, in honor of your survival and the Dallas Cowboys playing this Sunday, I thought we'd do a tailgate BBQ after my service." Rev. Carter smiled.

"That sounds great. Where and what BBQ?" "The dining hall said they would cook it for us." "And who's paying for that?" Karl grunted.

"Why, the congregation, of course," Rev. Carter answered.

"We have to pay for our own lunch?"

"We can go over the details later." Rev. Carter started to the door, but stopped and looked back at Karl. "And since when does coming to church one time make you the congregation? You know, going to a rodeo one time doesn't make you a cowboy." Rev. Carter laughed.

Karl followed him to the door and held it while they walked out, "No, but shooting one person does make you a murderer." He shut the door and walked back in the kitchen.

"Honey, why don't you get out and get some fresh air? You've been closed up in a hospital for two days," Betty suggested.

"Fine." He stood at the door long enough for the Carters to get on the elevator so he wouldn't have to talk with them. Slipping back into his jacket, he pushed the "down" button for the elevator. Once he made it outside, he looked around at the few people that were walking through the courtyard and others that were walking to the beach. He decided that he would ride to the beach and see how rough the waves were. Reaching in his pocket to make sure he had his key, he headed to the parking lot for the golf carts.

Chapter 37

Derrick sat at the breakfast table with the orientation trip while the ladies talked about their homes and the men fixated on Jaqs and anything she talked about. Looking at his phone Derrick still hadn't received a reply from Kat and lifting it above the table he typed, "Please answer me!"

A minute passed by and his phone buzzed with a message from Kat, "There isn't anything to talk about. Every time I turn my back you and Jaqs are together. I'm not interested in a rollercoaster relationship."

"I had no idea she was in my room. If I need to I'll fire her so you don't have to worry about her anymore." He typed back.

"And how is that going to look? It's best we call it quits. I have a call coming in I have to go." She lied.

Derrick placed his phone on the table and took a sip of his coffee, "What do you have planned for us today?" A lady pulled him out of his trance.

"We are going on down the Mississippi River on a paddle wheel boat."

"Well, I'm ready. This place has an electrical problem, my light kept turning on in the middle of the night. We better leave before it burns down." An elderly man threw his napkin in his plate. Derrick chuckled inside thinking back when Jack and Gerald had put their lamp on the roof to keep the ghost from turning it on. A secret he left out with this group.

Simon stood from the table and excused himself as a few other followed suit, Jaqs turned to Derrick, "Everything ok back at CBC?"

"Yeah, Betty had a mild heart-attack but she's back and doing ok."

"I'm sorry for causing trouble with Kat, it won't happen again." She assured him.

Not buying the remark, "Thanks."

"I am going to head upstairs for a bit." She smiled at Simon who was standing by the stairs with a guilty expression.

Derrick's phone buzzed again this time a message from the director, "Have we had any theft problems since I've been gone?"

"No, why? What happen?"

"I'll explain later." She answered then turned to the police officers and Karl, "No, we haven't had any problems."

"I still don't know why a thief would take the one cart with no accessories on it." One of the police officers said.

"Because they don't want all that crap to make it look like it came from the hood!" Karl huffed. The one white police officer turned and smiled at the black officer.

The director quickly jumped in, "And you have looked around the campus to make sure you didn't park it somewhere else or someone moved it?" The words crossed her lips before she realized the can of worms she opened. "Forget!" Karl's voice climbed two octaves. "I might mix up my meds occasionally, but I'm not going to forget where I parked. And no, nobody just used it. I lock it up."

He pointed at the lock on the ground.

"Someone definitely used bolt cutters on it," one of the officers said to the director. A light went off in Karl's head, and he walked over to Violet's ATV and tried to open the tool box she had locked in the back of her ATV. "And I know who cut it!" Karl exclaimed like a detective solving a case. The two officers and the director turned their attention to him and waited for the rest of the story. Karl started to share that Violet had bolt cutters when he saw Jack peer around the building waving and signaling not to say anything. "Well?" One of the officers said.

"Hang on." Karl answered and pushed his way through the threesome toward Jack. "Did you have something to do with this?" he asked, disappearing from the group around the building.

"No," Jack answered. "Violet?"

"I don't know, but the last thing I need is the police snooping around her apartment."

"Why would you care if she has a winery and armory? If she took my golf cart, she needs to pay!" He tried to turn and return when Jack grabbed his arm and pulled him back.

"I am kinda in business with Violet, and if she gets busted, then I get busted," Jack pleaded.

Karl rolled his eyes and shook his head. "You owe me a golf cart!" He pointed at Jack, then ducked back around the building. "I'm going to my apartment. Find my damn cart!" he yelled back at the director and officers. "We keep all the paper work on the golf carts in my office," the director replied, leading the officers across the courtyard while a nervous Violet watched from her balcony.

Jack and Karl climbed in Jack's golf cart and started to back out when Karl looked at his steering wheel. "You have controls for your radio on the steering wheel? You're becoming a millennial!"

"What?" Jack laughed.

"That's what's wrong with this generation, too damn lazy to do anything. Technology is killing everyone."

"What are you talking about?"

"Just drive." Karl looked at the custom wooden bar mounted between the seats and noticed his bourbon bottle was missing. "Where's the bottle?"

Jack thumbed behind him. "Back there."

Karl turned and looked at a box with a few glasses and two bottles of bourbon, "You expect me to reach back there for the bottle?"

"No, I wouldn't want to inconvenience you," Jack laughed and grabbed the bottle, pouring a shot for both of them. "We are starting early, aren't we?"

"Don't preach, just drive!" They started to leave when Rev. Carter walked by, and Karl held up his glass toasting him. "Here's to your tailgate this Sunday."

Jack looked back at Rev. Carter staring at them. "You just toasted a preacher at 10 a.m.!"

"It'll give him something to pray about," Karl replied, pointing to the beach.

Chapter 38

Karl pouted the rest of the day; he wouldn't speak to anyone at lunch or supper and even skipped his chocolate cake and turned in early. He had lived in the South most of his life, had never had anything stolen from him, and it was the last thing he thought would happen at CBC. Little to Betty's knowledge, he was planning on moving, but even if she wasn't aware, it was a threat she had heard a hundred times since they had moved in.

The following morning, with little sleep, Karl fixed a cup of coffee and wandered out onto the balcony. Jack was already in his chair reading the paper as Karl sat on the other side of the railing pulling out all the ads. "I don't know why they want to litter a paper with so much crap!"

Without looking, Jack answered, "You could download in on your iPad and forego all the ads."

Karl shot him a disguised look. "And join the lazy millennial group? No thanks!"

The sun had already been working on topping the other buildings at CBC, and as the rays broke out onto the balconies, the two men blocked it with their papers. A light wind blew the steam from both cups as both Karl and Jack took a sip at the same time. Betty looked through the sliding glass doors, giggling over the two drinking at the same time, turning their paper at the same time, and even crossing the same leg.

The sound of a large truck pulling in behind the office caught Karl's attention, and he folded his paper down to catch the glimpse of the truck hauling a golf cart. He craned his neck up to get a better look, but after closer inspection he settled back down in his chair, "Some jackass had his golf cart pimped out like yours." He went back to his paper.

Jack nonchalantly peeked around his paper at the truck, a smile forming across his face, "Yep, that lucky jackass." Snickering, he went back to reading his paper.

Violet was impatiently waiting at the golf cart parking for the truck to pull around and park. As the young man jumped out of the cab, he yelled over the truck engine, "Hello, Mrs. Violet, what do you think about the cart!"

Violet waved her hands down. "Not so loud, we got to hurry and get this thing off!"

"What's the rush?" "I stole it."

The young man started to laugh, but noticing her serious expression, he swallowed the lump that had formed in his throat and without any questions quickly unloaded the cart. He handed her the receipt and the owner's manuals to the new stereo, light bar, and the massive speaker system. As the truck peeled out leaving the parking lot, Violet smiled at the custom racing stripes, newly upholstery seats, seventeen-inch tires with spinning chrome hubs, and the steering wheel like Jack's.

The young driver had also left Violet her new gun rack for the back of her side by side, and looking at the package, she wondered how hard it was to install it herself. She had planned on Simon doing it for her, but since she figured out a way to drive to the local shooting range without getting on the road, she was hell-bent to do it herself.

Violet threw the box in the back of her side by side and jetted toward the office, where she found the director standing in front with a puzzled look. "What's with the look?" Violet greeted her.

"Kinda early to be out riding, isn't it?" she asked.

Violet looked around the campus, then back at the director, "If these people aren't up, you need to call the coroner. Can I use the tools in the maintenance shop?"

"Sure, the men are probably already there. You're working on your ATV?"

Violet pushed her helmet over her head and flipped up the visor. "Yep, putting on my gun rack!"

As the dust cleared from Violet's ATV, the director saw Kat walking up the path in aerobic pants and tank top shirt, "Wasn't your opinion that Jaqs wasn't wearing enough clothes?"

"My complaint is that she flirts with the residents." "Isn't that flirting?" The director pointed at her attire. "No, it's fitness class," Kat answered, noticing two board members walking up with another sharply dressed man.

"Good morning! I wasn't expecting board members today," the director greeted them.

"It wasn't on our agenda either, but with the resort next door pushing the issue of claiming our beach property, we need to put something together. This is one of the attorneys we have hired to represent us," one of the board members replied.

"Represent?" Kat asked.

"Good morning, Kat, looks like we are going to court over the issue. Can we meet inside?" He opened the door, then looked at Kat, who was heading to her class. "We need to ask you a few questions too," he waved Kat in.

After sitting in the boardroom and going over the laws concerning beach property, the attorney explained that the resort was claiming that they had been in business for twenty-five years and had always used the space.

"I don't understand—if CBC has always owned the property and paid taxes, then it's ours, isn't it?" Kat asked. "They are trying to use land grab as a means to acquire the property. It won't happen, but as long as they fight it, we have the expense of defending it. Kinda like bullying," the attorney explained.

"I'm sorry, but what do you need me for?" Kat asked, still standing behind one of the leather chairs. The two board members smiled, then looked at the attorney

Chapter 39

"We shouldn't have to wait in line," Karl griped, looking at the breakfast line. "Sweetie, if it wasn't any good, we wouldn't have to wait. There's a good thing about lines." Betty tried to add some positive insight to Karl, who was still fuming about his cart being stolen.

"There's nothing ever good about a line," he replied, looking ahead. "Just get the damn eggs and move on!" he yelled at a lady who was having a hard time deciding. After a dirty look and decisions made, Karl filled his plate with eggs, bacon, and biscuits and gravy. He grabbed two glasses, then looked back at Betty, who was talking with the lady behind the buffet. Impatiently, he headed to their normal table.

"Where's Betty?" Jack asked, already sitting and eating.

"Who knows?" Karl salted his plate, arranged their glasses then grab extra bacon for his plate.

A lady wearing an oversized beach hat and Hawaiian shirt stopped by their table. "Are you gentlemen coming to the beach party today at lunch?"

"Parties are for night! This is just lunch on the sand," Karl complained with a mouth full of bacon.

Jack laughed. "He said yes."

"Can I put you down for bringing something?" The lady asked.

Karl almost spit out his bacon, "Bring? I moved to this place so I didn't have to worry about cooking. If people are cooking and bringing their food, you can count me out!" "Put him down for chocolate cake," Jack smiled at her. She smiled back, checking off Karl's name for a cake. Karl pulled her clipboard down to look what she wrote, then went back to his breakfast, muttering, "Don't hold your breath."

Violet and June walked up with their trays in hand and volunteered after hearing the lady ask. "Put us down for wine." Violet pushed her way to the table.

"Oh, I'm sorry. This isn't a drinking party." "What kind of party is it?" Violet looked at her.

"Well, I'm Southern Baptist, and I believe if you drink you'll go to hell. What else would you like to bring?" She innocently smiled at Violet, who was now speechless with her mouth wide open.

"Boy, it's tough to silence her. You better put us down for deviled eggs and Angel Food Cake," Jack grinned.

"Oh, I love Angel Food Cake. The last time we had it was when that young gentlemen came to the house and—" June answered, but was interrupted by Violet.

"I know more Southern Baptists that drink than Catholics," Violet said, eyeing down the lady.

Rev. Cater and Diana walked by with their food, "Hey, Reverend, if we drink, are we going to Hell?" Karl blurted out.

"Fine! Don't come." The lady was tired of putting up with them and moved on. Violet and Karl laughed, leaving the Reverend to wonder why he was asked. Betty returned to the table with only one small plate and her typical glass of ice tea.

"Chocolate pie?" Jack asked, looking at her plate. She smiled. "Don't judge me."

Thirty minutes later, Betty was still talking about the pie while she and Karl headed to their apartment, holding hands. They cut across the courtyard and past the golf cart parking to find another cart in Karl's parking spot. Betty patted his arm. "Don't get upset. If they don't find your cart, the insurance company has assured me they will replace it."

Karl looked at the cart in his space. "I'm not upset. But whoever the smuck is that has to drive this cart should be." He grinned at Betty and continued walking, "And it better be out of my spot by noon," he added.

Lunch time had come before they realized it, and with Betty still fixing her hair, Karl yelled from the kitchen that it looked fine and for them to go. He walked out to the balcony to see a sea of people making their way to the beach. Violet cleared the bridge as she roared across the wooden and concrete structure, followed by Rev. Carter and Diana in the cart that had been parked in his space.

Figures! he thought.

Betty walked out with a flowered blouse and knee-length khaki shorts. "You ready?" she asked, holding a red-tinted straw hat.

Karl walked back in, observing, "You're taking a hat. It took you twenty minutes to fix your hair." He received a light giggle for his comment and ignorance, and together they stepped in the elevator and rode down to the lobby. The doors opened to Jack, who was wearing his signature white slacks and fedora hat, lighting a cigar.

He immediately extinguished it on the bottom of his boat shoes. "Sorry, Betty, do you guys want to ride in my cart?"

"Sure, and you didn't have to put that out on my account. But thank you." She patted him on his shoulder. Karl and Betty climbed in the back seat of Jack's golf cart, and as if being chauffeured, they rode to the beach holding hands. Jack stopped long enough for Kat to jump in with them, and the four of them topped the bridge to white tents, chairs, and a long table covered with the best food CBC offered.

"Wow!" Jack said, surprised at the spread.

"Only the best for you guys," Kat playfully elbowed him in the side.

As Jack's cart came to a rest in a parking spot, Karl noticed Jack crossing his fingers, and showing Kat; before he could ask what that was for, Violet pulled him out of the back seat. "What are you doing?" he asked her, then noticed everyone standing around, ready for an announcement.

"I felt bad for the way I've treated you, and with Betty in the hospital, I wanted to do something," Violet explained. "Your golf cart wasn't stolen. I know you liked Jack's cart, so June and I had your cart customized!" She waved toward the golf cart that was parked on the sand, the massive stereo speakers blaring out Frank Sinatra's Come Fly With Me.

Karl's eyes grew wider than ever before, and the feeling that an elephant just sat on his chest caused his blood pressure to reach dangerous levels. Speechless, he looked at Betty, who tipped her ice tea toward him, then back to the cart sporting the racing stripes, big tires, and steering wheel that he was complaining about only a day earlier.

"He's speechless again! Twice in one day," Violet bragged.

"Why did you do this to my golf cart?" he squeaked out. ear.

"Just call it neighborly," Violet grinned from ear to Neighborly? That's not the first thing that comes to my mind. Has everyone gone mental? My cart! He fought to keep his thoughts inside. "I don't know what to say."

"Say 'Thank you.'" Betty pushed him to the cart and made him sit inside. He looked over the satellite radio and the switches not having a clue how to work anything. "These tires won't get stuck in the sand," Violet explained, leaning on the front of the cart and pointing down. Karl stuck out his bottom lip and shook his head in agreement. "And the light bar will light up anything on the beach, plus run off any teens necking." Karl tried to smile.

"Want to take it for a spin?" Jack asked, walking up. Karl looked at the people that had lost interest and formed a line adjacent to the tables. "After we eat." He climbed back out and looked at Violet, gathering up the strength to say "Thanks." A somewhat smile formed crookedly on his face. I hope I wake up from this damn dream, he thought.

"This doesn't mean we're dating." She pointed at him and joined June in line.

"Thank you," Betty whispered to him. "I was praying that you wouldn't flip out."

"I think I'm in shock," he whispered back. Betty laughed, not realizing he was being serious.

Chapter 40

After a sleepless night and an impatient morning waiting on the paper, Karl sat on the balcony with his coffee and half the paper scattered on the floor. Jack slid open his glass door and stuck his head outside. "Is it safe out here?" he asked.

He received a grunt for an answer and figured it wasn't a scream, so perhaps it was safe. Setting his paper on the table, he carefully eased back in his chair with a full cup of coffee, noticing half of Karl's paper on the floor with a few sections already blown over the railing. He started flipping through the paper as Karl grunted a few more times about something he was reading.

"Did you see this article on the college kids protesting about politics?" Jack asked, trying to get something out of him.

"Bunch of damn babies!" Karl barked. Jack smiled about getting some movement from Karl. "If they put half the time in something constructive as they do bitching about everything, they'd be worth something."

"Maybe so." Jack flipped pages.

Karl set his paper down and faced Jack. "A summer or two in the hay fields would shut them up. That's what's wrong with this generation—they want everything handed to them and don't want to work for it." Karl picked his paper up and then quickly dropped it, facing Jack again, "I say give them a damn M1 rifle and put them on the front line. After seeing their buddy's head blown off by some North Korean, they'd have a change of heart." He paused. "Protesting!?! It's called complaining and throwing a fit because you didn't get want you wanted!"

Jack started to question his plan to get Karl to talk. "Well, not much has changed. They protested in the 1960s too."

"The sixties!" Karl blurted out, causing Jack to spill his coffee. "They were protesting a war! It had meaning back then."

"So you protested in the sixties?"

Karl stared at him with one eye cocked, "Hell, no, I didn't protest!"

Betty slid open their glass door and stepped out. "I see you boys are solving the world's problems."

Karl went back to reading his paper. "The whole damn world is going to hell!" he grumbled.

"Good morning, Jack," Betty smiled and decided to step back inside. Jack gave her a small good morning wave.

"Speaking of guns, I told Violet I would walk down this morning." Jack set down his paper and climbed out of the chair.

"Hang on, I'll come with you," Karl said, following suit.

Jack paused for a brief second. "You sure? You guys had some pretty harsh words yesterday after lunch. Maybe we should wait till they get your cart back to normal."

"I don't want to sit around here all morning. I probably should apologize—the guy at the custom shop said for me to bring back the cart, and he can put everything back to normal." Karl walked in his apartment leaving Jack to wonder what he was really thinking. Apologize? Jack thought to himself.

On the ride down in the elevator, Jack noticed Karl wearing flip-flops and started to ask him about them, but the doors opened to Violet and June's floor before he had time. They stood in front of the door waiting for the other to knock. Karl looked at Jack with a puzzled look, then nodded toward the door for him to knock.

After a few soft knocks, Karl shook his head and banged on the door with the back of his fist. June opened the door. "Goodness, is there a fire?"

Karl barged in with "No! Where's Violet?"

June looked at Jack with a concerned look that caused Jack to rethink bringing Karl with him. "I'm right here!" Holding a 12 gauge shotgun, Violet stepped out of the room where she kept her wine.

"You can put down the gun; I'm here to apologize," Karl barked. Dead silence filled the room, making it look like a standoff, and waiting for an answer, Karl scanned the room looking for the real reason he came with Jack.

"OK? Apology accepted." Violet threw the shotgun on the couch. As the tension in the room lowered, Jack butted in with the reason for his visit: He and Violet had planned to move several cases of wine to a restaurant down the beach. While they planned their day, Karl spotted the item he had come for—Violet's keys to her ATV.

"Well, I apologized, so you guys can plan your bootlegging, and I'm heading to the diner," Karl blurted out, then bolted out the door, leaving everyone speechless again, not recognizing that he had pushed the down arrow on the elevator.

Karl happily threw the keys in the air and caught them as he walked out the lobby of the Towers and toward the parking lot of golf carts. The sight of his cart sitting in his space all pimped out turned his stomach and fueled his plot of revenge. The shop better hurry up and come get this thing, he thought. He stopped in front of Violet's ATV and examined how to open the small door. After a few tries, he climbed over and fell into the seats.

Pulling himself up in front of the steering wheel, he gave a quick rise of the eyebrows and inserted the key into the ignition. He turned the keys, gave the gas pedal a gentle push, and the beast awoke and grumbled throughout the buildings of CBC and the resort next door. A flock of seagulls flew off with the echoing sound of 110 horsepower of pure energy.

Two flights up in the Tower apartments, Violet's head craned up. "What is that?" she asked, walking toward her balcony.

"What is what?" June asked.

The three of them heard the revving of a 4-stroke engine outside, and Violet glanced at the countertop where she had left her keys, realizing they were now missing, "That son-of-a-bitch!" She grabbed the first gun close to the balcony door.

"Hang on, Violet!" Jack sprang forward, trying to wrestle the gun from the death grip she had on it.

"Is this part of your plan?" She glared at Jack. "Not at all—I had no idea."

The three of them scattered onto the balcony in time to witness Karl jet toward the bridge, half out of control and the other half scared to death. Karl aimed toward the bridge, and as he topped the concrete structure tires bounced off both sides, keeping Karl and the beast on the bridge before shooting out onto the beach.

Violet watched him disappear around the corner of the Towers. "That stupid jackass is going to kill himself." She paused, "Ha, this could be a good thing." She hustled back inside to grab her shoes and headed to the beach, followed by Jack and June. The three of them jumped in Jack's cart and followed the trail of destruction Karl had left.

Chapter 41

As Karl ramped the curb that separated CBC's golf cart parking and the quiet, pristinely white sandy beaches of Perdido Key, his body was thrown forward, causing his foot to slip off the gas pedal. The thought of flip-flops not being the best shoes to wear crossed his mind as his right flip-flop lodged itself around and behind the gas pedal. Karl fought to release the foot that was now holding the gas pedal to the floor while he tried to steer the 110 horsepower beast around innocent bystanders.

The howl of an elderly man screaming "OH SHIT" echoed throughout the sleepy community over the roar from Violet's ATV as Karl wiped out the few chairs from residents of CBC. As the scene unfolded in front of Jack, Violet, and June, who were watching from the bridge, there couldn't have been a better time for Hank to be inspecting his beach employees and visiting with his guests.

The colorful echoes of Karl's language caught Hank's attention while he straightened the last chair and umbrella on his side of the beach. As if playing out in a horror film, Hank looked around the last of the 40 beach chairs and down the line to see an ATV hurling his way, Karl's eyes as wide as his mouth. As a trail of chairs and umbrellas hurtled into the air behind Karl, Hank's panic took over, and he did the only thing he could think of—run.

The resort's beach crew watched as their boss, who was wearing his favorite three-piece suit, ran for his life, zigzagging down the white sandy beaches of Perdido Key. "I don't know about you guys, but this is the best entertainment I've had in my life," One of them said to the other. Hank took action to prevent being mauled by Karl, diving into the emerald waters of the gulf, allowing Karl to continue his destruction of the next four resorts' beach equipment.

Jack, Violet, and June sat in their golf cart with their mouths wide open, eyes fixed in the direction of the sunset as Violet's ATV vanished out of their sight. "Damn," Violet softly spoke.

"You can't make up a scene like this," June replied from the back seat. "Jack, drive down the street and let's see if we can see him," she added. Jack drove down the lane designated for bikes and joggers looking through the resorts that lined the gulf until they saw flashing red lights on the beach. Stopping, they looked at each other, then drove into the parking lot of a resort, leaving their cart and heading onto the beach.

They could hear Karl before they could see him in the middle of a pack of beach patrol ATVs and trucks. And as the trio came within sight, Karl pointed at Violet. "There she is, she owns this satanic death trap!" The pitch of his screams reached dangerous levels.

"Sir, it doesn't matter who owns the ATV. You can't be driving on private property," an officer said, trying to calm him down.

"My damn foot got stuck, or I would have stopped at our property line!"

Another officer interrupted, speaking to the first one. "Captain, there is a manager on the phone with 911 claiming his resort was targeted by this ATV."

The first officer looked at Karl. "Is this true?"

"That jackass was just in the way—I wasn't targeting him." Karl looked at the trio for help.

"You know this man?" The officer turned to them. "Yep!" Violet spoke up, "He's been plotting to kill ole Hank for over a week now." She grinned.

Karl almost passed out. "I have not!" his voice cracked and skipped.

"You gave him the ATV?" The officer asked.

Violet thought for a second of the corner she was backing herself in, then answered, "Nope, he stole it!"

The officer turned back to Karl, who was frozen with his mouth wide open. "Sir, we need to take you to the station to figure this out."

It took a minute to register with Karl. "You're arresting me?"

"You can't be terrorizing beach goers with an ATV." He looked at the other officer, adding, "Don't handcuff him."

"Jack, do something!" Karl said as the officer helped him out of the cart.

"Betty and I will be right there," Jack said as the officer helped Karl into the back seat of his four-door truck.

"Are you pressing charges for him stealing your ATV?" the officer asked Violet.

"Nah, can I drive it back to CBC?" "Drive slow." he instructed her.

Violet climbed in the ATV and fired it up as Jack and June walked back through the sand to Jack's cart. "I'm loving CBC more and more every day!" June giggled, climbing in Jack's cart.

The beach patrol truck passed them as they drove back to CBC, Karl's glare shooting daggers at them through the closed window. Violet obeyed the officer's instructions on going slow until they left the beach, and then she opened up the 4-stroke engine, spraying sand twenty feet behind her as she jetted toward CBC.

Jack thought about what he was going to tell Betty, and he came up with a half-dozen ways to break the news, but each one came across funny to him. After the news was broken to Betty and she had fixed her hair and ice tea, they walked to the office to let the director know. They met Kat on the walk to the office. "I heard Violet telling a group of people—is Karl OK?" she asked.

"I don't know; the last time Karl went to jail, he caused a ruckus in the cell," Betty nonchalantly replied.

"He's been to jail before?" Kat asked, surprised. "It's a whole 'nother story."

With the director gone, Kat drove Betty and Jack to the police station to bail Karl out. Walking into the station, they found Karl sitting in a chair beside a desk, giving the officer his side of the story. When the officer noticed the group, he excused himself, giving Betty a minute with Karl.

Kat and Jack sat in another set of chairs, giving him time to talk to her about Derrick. It had been a few days since the shower incident, but Kat was insistent that it was over between her and Derrick. This was something that Jack couldn't handle lightly, and he vowed a mission to get the two CBC love birds back together.

The voice of the officer interrupted their conversation. "I don't think Mr. Rutherfurd throwing a fit in a bakery has any relevance to this case," one officer told another, reading a report. Jack and Kat looked at each other in amazement that Karl had a record.

Chapter 42

In deep thought, Derrick stood staring into space over a counter at the Houston underground mall. The fight and break-up with Kat had eaten a hole in his gut, and he wasn't sure if he could handle any more of it. She has trust problems, he thought. Which could be from her previous boyfriend, but will that ever go away? And will the old boyfriend return again? The thoughts fought in his head to the point that he felt foggy.

So, none of this makes sense! He shook his head. A salesman stood across the glass counter with a smile on his face, "What do you think? Is this the one?" he eagerly asked.

Derrick stared into the carat-and-a-half diamond ring. "Yea, I believe this is the one." The words played over and over in his head: Just marry the girl!

"Shall we start an application for financing?" the salesman asked.

Pulling a credit card from his wallet, Derrick said, "No, this should cover it," handing the card to the salesman, who was wearing a bigger smile.

Derrick stuck the small bag that held the box and ring into his jacket pocket and headed to the food court. With a glance at his watch, he picked up his pace, knowing they would be waiting on him. Turning the corner and seeing a table with Jaqs, Simon, and a few of the people on the trip, he looked across the tables to see the three gentlemen chasing the sample trays. A smile formed on his face, thinking back of Jack and Karl doing the same thing.

"There's our fearless leader—where have you been?" Simon asked.

"Tell me we are going somewhere where I can relax. These malls are brutal," one of the ladies added.

Smiling, Derrick replied, "As soon as we can retrieve the men, we are heading to some low-key and relaxing cottages on the beach," he answered.

A paralyzing whistle stopped all movement in the mall. Derrick looked at the lady who had just asked him about relaxing, and she pulled her two fingers from her mouth. "Come on!" she yelled at the three men. Derrick had a flashback of Violet.

"Where in the world did you learn to whistle that loud?" Jaqs asked.

Innocently, she replied, "I was raised with four brothers." Jaqs smiled, not knowing why being raised with four brothers had anything to do with knowing how to whistle.

The three men joined them, each carrying an over abundant amount of free samples and a mouth full. As he climbed into the van, a secretive smile came across Simon, who had enjoyed the trip not having to unload at every stop to satisfied Violet's obsession about balancing everything. They drove through the city and to their final destination, the same two beach cottages that were always on their last stop.

As the group bypassed the cottages and made a beeline to the beach and calm waters of the gulf, leaving Simon with the van and luggage, his smile slowly disappeared. "The sound of the waves never gets old," one of the ladies observed.

"Our beach is prettier," one of the men replied.

"I am going to help Simon with the bags. We have a couple of hours before supper, so please take your time and enjoy the evening," Derrick said, then turned to Jaqs, "You want to stay here with them?" She returned his answer with a smile. Over the last few days Jaqs had taken a step back from pursuing Derrick, half embarrassed and the other half wanting to keep her job.

Derrick walked up on the front porch, where Simon had already separated the bags. "Let's bring those bags over here and put these over there," Derrick pointed to the bags Simon had placed on the other cottage.

Staring at Derrick with a blank look, Simon asked, "Are you serious?"

"No," Derrick chuckled, grabbed a couple of bags and took them inside.

That evening Derrick congregated everyone in one cottage and thanked them for a great trip, then led them out to the restaurant down the street. After instructing Simon to lead the group, he held back to bring up the rear, Jaqs staying back with him. Derrick shook his head, not at Jaqs but at the construction that was still taking place on the road. Getting close to a work crew, he recognized the foreman from the previous trip. "Still working late?" Derrick greeted him.

"Got to hurry up and finish it," the burly man answered, then looked at Jaqs. "What kinda of retirement home are you running? I want to put in my application now." He smiled and tipped his hardhat at Jaqs, who ate up the compliment.

Derrick laughed. "We'll take it."

"Are y'all trying to kill off the old men?" another construction worker asked, eyeing Jaqs.

The foreman threw his hardhat at him. "What kind of comment is that? Show some respect."

"Oh, it's OK, I like it," Jaqs answered with a Marline Monroe pose.

"I was actually talking about the man that died here on their last trip," the foreman replied.

Jaqs looked at Derrick. "Who died?"

"A good friend," he answered, waving at the construction workers, and caught up with the group.

Jaqs overheard another comment about wishing for a gust of wind as she caught up with the group, enjoying the stares. Once seated at the table, the group enjoyed an evening of fresh seafood, drinks, and company. The successful trip had added to the excitement of moving into CBC and meeting the residents for everyone.

Once done with supper, the group headed back to their cottages by the road. Derrick asked Jaqs and Simon to go with them so he could have some time on the beach. He stepped onto the dark beach with a few lights shining from the buildings illuminating the sand and small waves crashing onto the beach.

Derrick could make out a soft glow on the horizon where the moon was tracking its way up, but had not yet appeared. With a staggered walk in the deep sand, he pulled out the box and ring, looking at the sparse sparkle in the low light. He made his way to the area where Gerald had seen his last moonlight and had joined the love of his life. "Well, old friend, without you this wouldn't be possible," he said to himself and to Gerald. He took a deep breath and thought back on the advice: Just marry the girl.

He pulled out his cell phone and made a call. "Hello?" The voice on the other end answered.

"I am taking your advice," Derrick replied, looking at the ring.

"The best decision of your life. Where are you?"

"Actually sitting where Gerald took his last breath."

"Tell him hello for me," Jack replied, sitting on his balcony.

Chapter 43

The following morning, Jack was surprised to see Karl dressed for Sunday service when he came out on the balcony for coffee and the paper. Neither said anything to each other as Karl got settled in his chair with the Sunday paper. Tossing the advertisement sections to the floor, "Half the damn paper," he grumbled. "I see you're going to service this morning," Jack commented, never taking his eyes off his paper. "Didn't have a choice."

"Prison will change a man." Jack grinned at his paper. Karl ignored the comment and studied the paper, a cool wind blowing through the balconies of the Towers and causing both men to shiver. Both flipped pages simultaneously as if they were racing through the articles when both of them sat up at the same time. Jack beat Karl to the question: "Are you reading page 9?"

"The resort is suing CBC for beach space?" Karl looked at Jack. "You're a real estate man. Can they do that?"

Jack was studying the article. "According to this, they're claiming that according to an old law, a fence on a property line for seven years can become the new property line. I don't know."

Betty stuck her head out the door. "We need to be going."

Karl glanced at his Timex. "It doesn't start for another 10 minutes."

"I want to get a good seat," Betty answered.

"It's church! There are no good seats," he pleaded his case only to receive a stare and for Betty to disappear back inside. Karl mumbled a few words, but then like a ten- year-old boy, climbed out of his chair and pouted as he walked back inside.

"Tell the Rev hello for me," Jack said before Karl's door slammed shut.

As they rode the elevator down, it stopped on the second floor. Betty looked at Karl, who was already rolling his eyes. The doors opened to June and Violet. "Well, good morning. You look beautiful this morning! What's the occasion?" June stepped on the elevator.

"We are going to church."

"Oh, today is Sunday." June looked back at Karl and smiled. Violet stood outside the elevator door staring at Karl, who was staring back at her. The door slowly closed, with Violet choosing to use the stairs.

June stopped at the foot of the stairs to wait for Violet. "You guys have a good morning," June said. "Karl?" she added, and when Karl looked back at her, "Tell Him I said hi," June grinned and pointed up.

"I would, but I don't think we're on speaking terms right now," he replied and caught up with Betty, who was on her march to the chapel with ice tea in hand.

A line had formed outside the church as Rev. Carter greeted each person as the small crowd entered the chapel, Dianna standing beside him like the First Lady. A group of ladies eyed down Karl, then mumbled among themselves about the latest news on the residence's newest criminal. "Take a picture! It'll last longer," Karl barked at them.

They threw their noses up and marched into the chapel, bypassing Rev. Carter. "Why they did let you out? For good behavior?" he asked in a loud voice.

"Aren't you supposed to greet people as they leave?" Karl wanted to change the subject.

"If they don't like the message, they won't talk to me, so this way is easier. So, how was hard time? I see you have both hands, that's a good thing about being a thief in the twentieth century," Rev. Carter laughed.

"It's the twenty-first century, jackass."

Betty threw her elbow in Karl's side. "You can't call the preacher a jackass." She started blushing.

"Oh, don't worry about it, Betty. I've been called worse by other prisoners. You guys go in and find a seat. I'd stay away from the left side," he added, winking at Karl.

Karl walked in to find the left side of the church filled with CBC's finest gossips and the group of ladies, who were still eyeing him down. Betty started to slide in a pew on the right side, but Karl grabbed her arm and guided her to the third row on the left side and filed in beside four of the ladies. A gasp silenced the chapel from the ladies, and they rose up and stormed to the back pew, all of them puffed up like mad hens. Karl allowed his first smile of the morning.

Rev. Carter didn't wait long before he started beating on the pulpit, preaching from a passage in Old Testament. He wasn't five minutes into his message when Karl realized he was talking about stealing and the punishment that God delivers. The longer the message went, the madder Karl got as Rev. Carter would glance at him ever so often. Karl pulled out his phone and texted Jack. "This jackass is preaching on stealing. Come get me, say it's an emergency."

A few minutes Jack texted back, "Sounds like a message you need to hear."

"Come get me!"

"I can't right now, in the library. Just fake a seizure. They'll either think you need medical attention or it'll give the rev a chance to cast out the demons."

"Thanks for no help." Karl sent back and started to put his phone back when another message buzzed. Jack sent a picture with him seating on the toilet and the caption "busy here" under the picture. A noisy lady sitting behind Karl gasped at the sight of Jack's pants at his ankles and the grin he was wearing.

Karl turned in his seat to see the commotion. "You should be ashamed of yourself for having a picture like that in church," she scolded him.

Karl hung his phone over the pew to show the picture, "Of this?" The next four rows behind the lady all gasped for air.

Betty elbowed Karl again. "You're going to get us kicked out of church," she whispered emphatically.

"I wish," he answered, turning to find Rev. Carter giving him a dirty look for interrupting his service.

Rev Carter closed his service with an unusual benediction; he stood in front of the congregation and pulled off his oversized black robe, revealing a Dallas Cowboys jersey. "Upon the request of many of our good people," he explained, "we are going to dismiss to a first- time tailgate party. I hope you can find it in yourselves to forgive others and enjoy true community." He raised his hand and dismissed everyone. Karl managed to slip out, missing conversation with Rev. Carter, and found Jack standing in the line for BBQ.

"You don't go to church, but you show up for the food," Karl grumbled, cutting in line with him.

Jack smiled. "Can't be seen with a criminal."

Karl smiled back, adding, "Trust me, they saw you." Jack gave him a puzzled look back.

Chapter 44

It wasn't long before Karl's news about being in jail became old news as the rumors spread through the tailgate party about the article on CBC being sued for beach property. Betty and Karl sat at a table covered with football decorations and BBQ, and every time someone would ask Karl about his arrest, he would quickly change the subject to the law suit, adding a few false pieces of information just to add fuel to the fire.

Kat walked up wearing an Atlanta Falcons jersey. "How are you guys doing?"

Karl gave her a funny look. "You know they aren't playing today." He pointed at her jersey with a half-eaten rib.

"But they host Monday night football, and I'll be cheering them on," she smiled.

"What happened to the good ole days when football was just on Sundays? Now it's Monday night, Thursday night, some on Friday—the media is flooding the networks with football," Karl complained, shoving another rib in his mouth.

Jack set his plate down on the table, asking, "Why are you complaining? You don't even watch football." In response, Karl rolled his eyes and grabbed another rib.

"Well, I personally think football is a barbaric sport." Violet sat down across from Karl, who almost chocked on his rib.

Karl's first thought was the audacity of Violet sitting at the table with him, and the second . . . well, his mind couldn't leave the first thought. "What are you doing? And what are you talking about? You killed your attorney!" Everyone sitting within twenty feet stopped eating and faced their table. Claiming that someone killed their attorney is a crazy remark for most people, but the captive audience was looking at Violet, and after six months of living with her, nobody put anything past her.

"Why don't you announce it to the whole community?" Violet shot back at him. "And you're one to talk—you have a record!"

Kat quickly jumped in. "Maybe we should separate until everyone cools down."

"Sweetheart," June started, "It's going to take one of them to kick the bucket first. And at this rate, they're liable to outlive us all."

"Say! Isn't Derrick coming back this afternoon?" Violet asked Kat.

"Yes," she answered, thinking she'd rather watch Karl and Violet fight than talk about Derrick.

"You two need to hurry up and get married and have babies before mother earth comes for me," June innocently smiled.

Both Kat and Rev. Carter, who were eavesdropping from behind, spit out their food on the table. Kat wiped her mouth. "Actually, Derrick and I have decided to take a break."

Everyone sat at the table staring at her until Violet spoke up. "From what?"

"Things are just not working out right now. Let's change the subject," she asked.

"Is it that hottie from Brazil?" another man who was eavesdropping asked. Kat looked around and realized she had a captive audience of six tables.

"Leave the girl alone and mind your own business," Jack spoke up to everyone. The conversation went back to Karl and his night in jail. Kat was pleasantly surprised at their quick change in subjects and looked at Jack mouthing the words, thank you.

Jack got up to throw away his plate and whispered in Kat's ear, "But I seriously believe you need to hear him out when he gets here."

"I'm not sure I'm ready," she quietly replied.

Jack looked over the table at the white van pulling up to the visitor center. "You might want to make up your mind sooner than you think." He nodded in the direction of the van.

Damn, she thought. She hesitated before getting up, said goodbye to everyone, and headed toward the parking lot. Looking back, she saw Jack and Sylvia walking to her apartment and shook her head. Fumbling for her keys, she had started to unlock her car when the Director pulled up and stopped her.

"I need to see you before you go." "Can it wait until tomorrow?"

"Nope. Follow me back to the office." She flung her purse over her shoulder and started her march to the offices. Kat followed a few steps behind her, thinking of what she was going to say to Derrick if they ran into each other. Walking through the luggage and people who were on the trip, she didn't see him and was starting to feel relieved when she walked into the office and literally ran into him.

"Sorry," he said, looking as surprised as Kat.

"It's OK." She pushed by him and followed the director.

"This involves you too, Mr. St. Clair," the director said, waving him in with them.

Derrick and Kat stood in front of the desk apart from each other while the director put away her things. "Seriously?" she began, "You two are going to have to work something out. I can't handle all this drama."

"Drama?" Kat asked in an annoyed tone.

The director put her hand up. "That's not what I want to talk about. The board is meeting here tomorrow morning, and I need both of you here. Dressed professional," she added, looking at Kat.

Derrick drew back at the comment, thinking Kat always dressed professionally. "Is that what you needed to tell us? I still have to debrief our folks and get them settled."

"Yes." She pointed her finger at them. "No emotions or relational problems. We don't need to add anything to our problem with this law suit."

Kat walked out first and tried to get out before Derrick stopped her, but as the door was shutting in front of him, he opened it and called her name. Kat stopped and turned with her hand on her hip. "What?"

"We have to talk this through," he pleaded.

"There isn't anything to talk about. Obviously I can't handle jealousy, and obviously you don't know the boundaries of women."

He gripped the small box in his pocket. "You have nothing to be jealous about. I explained to Jaqs that her job was on the line and there was nothing between us."

"And I'm sure she took it to heart," Kat answered sarcastically and turned, walking through the courtyard with the small koi pond.

"Kat?" Derrick jogged after her, pulling out the box. "No," Kat answered, never turning around and seeing what was in his hand. Derrick stood watching her zig-zag through the azaleas and pick up to a jog, making her way to her vehicle with tears flowing.

Chapter 45

D
riving over the bridge leading to the beach, June almost broke her arm waving at Kat, who was trying to get in her car for a second time before someone else stopped her. Kat gave a half-hearted wave back, then ducked into her car to start the engine. June tried to turn and see her back out, but with Violet's driving, they were over the bridge in a flash of an eye. "You don't have to drive like a bat out of hell all the time," June suggested, pushing her grey hair out of her face.

Violet looked at her through her white helmet. "What's the purpose of having horse power if you're not going to use it?" And without letting up, she ramped the curb separating the parking lot and the beach as the few people scattered throughout the beach turned their attention to the sisters.

Violet pulled her ATV up feet from where the wet sand met the dry white sand, and once the engine was shut off, everyone on the beach took a breath of relief and went back watching the sun dip into the Gulf of Mexico. June stretched her head and took in a deep breath of salt air as a light breeze met them. Hanging her helmet behind her, Violet noticed a sharply dressed man walking their way.

"Here comes frizzle britches."

June turned to see Hank walking through the sand in his Italian leather shoes. "You need to take off those shoes and let your feet enjoy the sand," she said, greeting him from a short distance.

"I don't want to take a chance of someone stealing them! Been a lot of crime here in the last six months."

"You could have left them with your boyfriend," Violet replied, looking out over the gulf.

Hank placed his hands on his hips. "I'm not gay!" Violet turned to him and looked him up and down.

"Keep telling yourself that," she answered in a lower tone. "I came to talk business," he responded, trying to change the subject.

"Pull up some sand and enjoy the sunset with us," June smiled at him.

"Don't have time. I can watch another one tomorrow." June faced the setting sun. "When you get our age, you take what you can get because tomorrow might not come."

Hank rolled his eyes. "Fine! As long as we can talk about an order I need."

A middle-aged couple walked past the three of them, wondering what two older ladies were doing in a souped-up ATV talking to a younger man in an Armani suit. The man waved as his wife gave an innocent smile, and June repaid the welcome with a smile and nod.

"You just ordered several cases the other day; have you gone through it already?" Violet asked.

"It seems that your wine is a hit among the tourists and a few locals. What would it take for my resort to be the exclusive restaurant to your wine?" Hank ran his hand through the soft sand.

"I'll have to talk to my business partner."

"Business partner?" both Hank and June asked simultaneously.

"Jack," she answered.

June pulled herself out of the ATV. "So that's what you guys have been sneaking around about?" She stretched her arms.

Hank stood up without brushing the sand off him and faced the ATV. "I believe we could both make a lot of money, and you wouldn't have to worry about taking it far."

Violet didn't say anything and looked forward, thinking about the offer. Hank was standing his ground watching her think when he felt something on his butt. He turned his head just in time to see June's hand brush over his butt again, and he quickly jumped to the side. "What are you doing?" he asked, his voice shooting up.

"Brushing your suit off—stand still." She tried to continue, but met resistance from him.

"I'm good," Hank insisted, his voice still in a high-pitched tone.

"You sound like Karl when he gets upset," June smiled.

"You sure you're not gay?" Violet cocked her head. "Just think about it." He stormed back to the resort, brushing himself off and straightening his jacket.

"That poor young man is wound tighter than an eight-day clock," June observed, watching him walking off.

Violet didn't reply and just continued watching the horizon, not really paying any attention to the sun or to Hank, who was still fighting the sand in his shoes. "I'm sorry," she said.

June looked back at Violet, "For?" She wasn't sure she really wanted to know why her sister was apologizing.

"For not being a good sister."

June squinted her eyebrows and waited for something else, but after a short moment, added, "Why are you say that? You have been a great sister . . . wait! You're not dying, are you?"

"No, stupid, I'm not dying." Violet patted the seat, hinting for June to sit beside her. After June climbed back in, Violet grabbed her hand, refusing to look at her. "You said in a blink of an eye, all this could be gone. I want to confess something, but I don't want you to make a big deal out of it."

"OK?" June questioned. "I'm afraid of dying."

"I think everyone is afraid of dying," June started to reply, but was cut off by Violet.

"But everyone else seems to have some sort of idea of what is beyond death." She looked at June. "I don't. I don't know what to think or believe. Nothing makes sense to me." June started to talk, but Violet cut her off again. "I don't need an answer, just for you to listen." June tightened her lips. "Gerald passed away on that beach in a peaceful way, believing he was joining his wife Doris. Betty has some weird sense of peace too, and Jack . . . well, I'm not sure he gives a crap. What if there isn't anything beyond this life for me?"

June tightened her grip on her sister's hand. "I believe that whoever or whatever created us doesn't plan for our life to end here. Whether we end up in heaven or ghosts roaming around, I believe our souls go with us and we have the choice to be happy."

"What about God?"

June glanced out into the distance as the sun touched the water. "I don't know."

Chapter 46

After a sleepless night of tossing and turning, Kat managed to scarf down a bagel and pour a cup of coffee before heading to work. Pulling into the parking lot, she spotted Derrick turning in and slowed down, allowing him time to park and start his walk to the office before she climbed out of her car. With her bag getting caught on the seatbelt, she gave it a hard tug, causing it to come shooting out her door and flinging past her, coming to a crash on the pavement in front of a well-dressed man wearing sunglasses and carrying a brief case. Her first thought was a new attorney for CBC.

The man leaned over and picked up her bag, "Did this bag do something to you?" he grinned.

She took it from him, "No, just one of those mornings.

Thank you," she replied and started back to her car.

"You don't remember me, do you?" he said, standing in the same spot.

Kat turned and looked at him with not a clue. "I'm sorry," she replied. He removed his sunglasses, and then Kat realized it was Gerald's grandson, whom she had met at the funeral. "Evan, right?" she asked.

He held out his hand. "You do have a good memory. How are things going, with the exception of this morning?" He smiled, showing his snow-white teeth.

"Things are good. Are you one of the attorneys?" "No, I'm here to talk with the board about the beach space that the resort next door is trying to claim."

"Well, I believe I have to be in that meeting. Would you like to walk with me? I promise not to hit you with my bag," she replied.

He laughed and gestured the way with his hand. "How are things with you and . . . I can't remember his name, the assistant director here."

"Derrick, and we are no longer together." It was hard for her to hear the words.

"I'm sorry," he replied from behind her.

She pulled open the door and returned his casual hand wave. "After you." She followed him into the foyer that was already filled with board members, a few staff, and Derrick, who was standing in the back. She stayed close to Evan, making it apparent that she came with him. Derrick didn't like what he saw.

The director called for everyone to join her in the conference room, which had been set up with papers in front of each chair. After everyone got settled, she announced, "Thank you for coming this morning. I am going to turn this over to our board chairman."

A man with a dark blue tie stood up. "Thank you! Many of you know that we have a court date set for the property dispute on the beach. The resort next door is fighting to take over ownership through an old, outdated law. Though we believe 100% that we would win in a court of law, we believe that our quirky manager would still give us problems. And as you might know, we have many residents that this dispute causes stress and some that love to retaliate." He took a swig of water, then continued, "So Mr. Harriman believes he has a solution. If you are not familiar with Mr. Harriman, he is the grandson of Gerald Harriman and is now the president of their company."

Evan stood up. "Thank you, and please call me Evan; my father is Mr. Harriman." He glanced at Kat, whose eyes caught his attention and caused him to stutter. "I believe the property next door would make a good investment, and as of 5:00 p.m. yesterday afternoon, we put in a bid to become the sole owners of the resort."

His remark caused many of the board members to straighten up in their chairs with smiles forming across the face of everyone. "Wow," the director said out loud.

"Now, there is a lot of paperwork to do and many variables that will have to come into play, but this not only forestalls any court hearings, but would put us in control of all the beach space. I ask that you keep this here until we have time to finish the buy."

The chairman stood back up. "We feel that this will take place in the next couple of weeks." He turned toward the director, adding, "We know you want to retire, but would you be willing to take over the resort for the first two years before leaving us?"

The director tried to swallow. "Yes, but what about CBC?"

The chairman turned to Derrick. "Are you ready to become the director?"

The question took Derrick by surprise, but he managed a squeaky "Sure."

"Very well, let's meet back here in two weeks to celebrate." The room broke out into a joyful conversation and congratulations for the director and Derrick. Derrick glanced over the table at Kat a few times, watching her talking to other board members before making his way around the table.

Before he could reach her, Evan stepped in. "I hope this is good news for you," he said to Kat. "My grandfather seemed to like you, and I doubt any of this would be happening without your persuasion."

"I'm sure everything would have happened without me," she downplayed the compliment. Derrick appeared to their side, and Kat looked at him with a curt "Congratulations."

"Yes, congratulations! I know you will be great in a director's position," Evan added and shook his hand.

"And how would you know that?" Derrick looked at Evan.

Evan took the hint. "I know good leadership when I see it. Have a great day," he said and started to turn, smiling to Kat as he said goodbye.

"What was that? He was complementing you," Kat asked, clearly more annoyed.

Derrick tried to defend himself, but Kat quickly walked out without giving him time. He followed her out into the lobby, where Violet stopped him. "Just the person I'm looking for," she said, cutting him off.

He looked over her shoulder at Kat disappearing out the door. "What can I do for you?"

"The director said to talk with you about changing apartments."

"Apartments? Where are you wanting to move to?"

"Sixth floor."

Derrick looked over the housing chart and noticed that the only apartment vacant on the sixth was above Karl and Betty. "You sure this is a good idea?" He looked at Violet.

"And why wouldn't it be?"

"You and Karl don't exactly see eye to eye."

"I won't be looking at him eye to eye—he'll be looking up at me," she smiled.

Chapter 47

As an excited group of board members thinned out of the offices and Kat walked out with Evan creating small talk, Derrick was filled with mixed emotions. Part of him wanted to storm out and snatch up Kat, and the other part of him wanted to punch Evan in the face. Needless to say, when Jaqs walked in smiling at Derrick, she hadn't a clue of the fire storm she was about to meet.

"Is the director here? She wanted to see me," Jaqs asked Derrick.

Before Derrick could answer, and probably a good thing, the director walked out of the board room. "Good morning, Jaqs, let's meet in my office. You too," she pointed at Derrick.

Oblivious to the trouble she had created, the board members still lingering around the office went out of their way to say hello. After a few handshakes and one questionable hug, Jaqs walked in the director's office and sat in one of the leather-backed chairs. The director closed the door with Derrick still standing, and she motioned for him to have a seat. "Jaqs, I take it that you have read the employee's handbook?"

Clueless, Jaqs answered, "Yes."

"Then you know it is against the rules to fraternize with other employees of CBC?"

"I read something like that."

"The display of affection you have shown toward Derrick has not only caused him problems with Kat, but has become a topic here, something I don't want." The director was surprising Derrick with her quick actions.

"I don't think—"

The director cut her off. "Wait till I am finish." Derrick tried to hold back his smile. "I have dismissed your flirting with men and the revealing clothes you wear, but actions toward someone that works here, especially when you know they are dating someone, is crossing the line. I am putting you on probation." Jaqs tried to say something, but the director cut her off with her hand. "Stay on course with your job, and if there is any further inappropriate behavior I will let you go. I am noting this conversation for your file. Any questions?"

Jaqs sat back in her chair, "So if I become a contracted employee, I can date whoever I want?" she snarled at both the director and Derrick.

The director smiled. "And if you bring 28 million to CBC, then I am sure we can accommodate you, too.

Close the door on your way out." She pointed to the door. Jaqs flipped her hair and walked out mad. "Are you good?" the director asked Derrick.

"I will be."

"Good, now go make up with Kat and get on with life. We have a lot to do here."

Derrick left the office and walked outside with a sense of relief that Jaqs wouldn't stir up anything else. He walked toward the art center seeing Jack disappear into the Loft Apartments and Jaqs heading to the back parking lot, where he thought she went to cool off.

But Jaqs didn't stop in the back parking lot—she crossed the property line, storming right into the offices of the resort. A surprised look came from Hank, who was talking with his secretary. "Can we help you?" he asked.

"Are you the manager?" "I am."

"Can we talk?" She barged into what she thought was his office.

Hank looked at his secretary. "I'll be right back." He disappeared into his office, shutting the door behind him. The secretary cocked her head and lifted an eyebrow before picking up her phone and sending a text. "Your fitness instructor is in the office with Hank."

"Really? Let me know if you learn why. And Thanks." Derrick texted back.

"So, do you still have an opening here?" Jaqs asked Hank. Little to anyone's knowledge, Hank and Jaqs had struck up a conversation weeks earlier after she was led to be a decoy for the folks at CBC.

He sat in his chair playing with a pen in his hands. "Yes," he replied, "but I think it might be more beneficial for the both of us if you stay with CBC during this time as we acquire their property on the beach."

Jaqs pulled herself up on his desk in front of his chair, crossed her legs, and flipped her hair back. "And what would I get out of it?"

Hank's heart skipped a few beats. "I'm sure we can work something out. I could use someone on the inside. But now is not a good time; why don't you come back over tomorrow evening after hours, and let's talk about our plan?"

"I can't wait." She stood up and walked out, leaving Hank in his chair.

His secretary watched Jaqs walk out, then leaned in Hank's door. "Everything OK?"

"Yes," he answered, not looking at her.

"Do you want to come back in here and let's finish the budget?"

He looked at her with a blank stare. "Give me a second." He continued to flip the pen in his hand.

Jaqs stormed back across the parking lot, running into Karl and Betty, "Hello, Rutherfurds," she said, but didn't stop.

Karl spun around in a circle trying to see who spoke with them and caught a glimpse of her as she rounded the corner. "What was that about?" he asked Betty.

"Just Jaqs being friendly." She climbed up in their golf cart with her ice tea.

Karl unplugged from the charger. "Time to take this blimp mobile back to the shop and get this crap taken off." He squealed the tires, sending Betty's head bobbling and spilling her ice tea.

Driving like a bat out of hell, Karl hit the shoulder of the highway and aimed toward the custom shop that had worked on his cart for Violet. He had made arrangements to have everything removed, and even though it was going to take 3-4 hours, he was bound and determined to wait.

Chapter 48

Violet and June were standing on the balcony when they spotted Karl and Betty cut across the bridge and down the highway on the designated shoulder for runners and bicyclers. "Where do you think they are going?" June asked.

"I don't know, but I have my suspicion." Violet walked inside and dialed the number to the custom shop. The young man that had helped her the first time answered, and after monetary persuasion he agreed to keep Karl and Betty there a little longer than they had planned. She then hung up with the custom shop and dialed the number for the movers she had hired and persuaded them to come right away and move their apartment while Karl was out. Within thirty minutes, the movers were knocking on their door. Violet had promised a hearty bonus, and the men began scrambling to move The Stevens Sisters four flights up. Jack walked in the foyer of the Towers whistling a Tony Bennett song, and jumping on the elevator, he pushed the sixth floor, only to stop on the second. Simon walked on backwards, carefully pulling a dolly with three five-gallon carboys of wine. "Where are you going?" Jack asked, moving out of his way.

"Six, please." He nodded toward the number pad on the elevator.

Jack pressed six. "Does Karl know yet?"

"No sir, he is at the custom shop having everything removed on his golf cart." The elevator stopped at the 5th floor. "Are you getting off?" Simon asked.

"Nope," Jack smiled. "I wouldn't miss this for the world." They rode to the sixth floor together, and Jack held open the door for Simon, seeing Violet in the living room ordering the movers around. "So, how are you going to break the news to Karl, and can I help?" He grinned.

Her first way of breaking the news startled Jack, and with his persuasion, they decided to be a little less shocking and break the news to Karl that night. Jack picked up on his whistling and headed back to the elevator, where the doors opened before he could press the button. Two men were in the elevator with half a dozen assault rifles and two dollies of ammo. "Don't let us frighten you. All this belongs to Ms. Stevens," one of them said.

Jack slipped on the elevator. "Son, once you have lived here a few months, the only thing that will scare you is the meatloaf." He tipped his hat at the men and rode down one flight.

Simon made another trip up with three more carboys and carefully set them in a rack that one of the moving men were in charge of assembling. "What does she do with all this wine?" he asked Simon.

"It's mostly a hobby . . . I think."

The man glanced in the living room and other men putting her gun collection on the walls. "She's got to be the coolest grandmother I've ever met," he replied.

Violet leaned in the door. "Grandmother?" "Do you have grandkids?" the man asked.

"Hell no, I ain't got grandkids," she blurted out. "Oh, sorry. Both my mother and my wife's mother have passed away, and we worry that are kids aren't getting the experience that most kids get with a grandmother," he replied, then went back to assembling another rack.

Violet rolled her eyes and walked in the room. "What does your wife do?"

The young man smiled at her question. "She works at a tackle store on the docks."

"She sells bait?"

"You could say that; they also have a small bar where many of the anglers get a drink after fishing all day."

"And you're not worried about those fisherman making a pass at your wife?" Violet pressed.

He laughed, "No, you'd have to meet her to understand why I'm not worried."

"Ugly, uh?"

He laughed harder, pulled out his phone, and showed Violet a picture. "Good Lord, she's gorgeous! Are these your kids?" Violet pointed at the picture.

"They are." He took back his phone.

"So what am I missing? She's beautiful and works at a bar. Those drunk fisherman are probably falling over themselves for her."

"Oh, they are. But she is as tough as her four brothers." He looked past Violet at her gun collection. "And she'd be jealous of your collection—she's a gun nut."

Kat walked in the open front door, saying, "Wow, you guys sure move fast." June sprung from the box she was unpacking and gave Kat a giant hug, pulling her from the front door to the living room. Violet gave her a tom- boy nod and went back to visiting with the young man and Simon.

Violet looked back out at the room. "How did you know we were moving?"

Kat smiled. "It's CBC! It's the new talk of the community."

"Us moving?" June asked.

"No, the reaction you are going to get from Karl." "Oh, we have plans for that announcement," Violet
   replied.

"Please go easy on him. He's a good guy," Kat defended Karl.

"Of course he's a good guy—it's one of the reasons we are moving above him. Plus if he wasn't married, she'd be jumping at the chance." June pointed at Violet.

Violet's expression turned. "What in the hell are you talking about? I'm single for a reason!"

June patted Kat on the shoulder. "I thinks it's the school yard girl being mean to the boy she really likes.

Look at these old photos I found." She pulled out a stack of photos.

"You've been smoking too much reefer if you think I like Rutherfurd!"

Kat laughed, then looked down at the photos June handed her—and almost dropped them looking at nude photos of June. "Goodness." She smiled at June.

"I used to have a body."

"I can see that," Kat blushed.

"Do you have any nude photos?" June asked. The men in the room got quiet and turned that attention to Kat, who was now three shades of red.

"No, I can't say I do."

"It's a good thing. I've heard that people steal pictures and plaster them on the lines," Violet said.

"On the lines?" Kat asked. "The internet!"

"Oh, online," she corrected Violet.

"That's what I said, on the lines." She waved in Kat's direction to end the conversation and went back to talking to the young man.

"Well, you need to take some nude photos before everything goes south," June whispered to Kat. "I'll help if you need a photographer."

"No! No! I'm good." Kat handed the photos back to

her.

Chapter 49

Karl parked his golf cart back in his spot four hours later, exhausted from their day and being mad the whole time. Jack strolled around the corner, stopped, then looked at Karl. "I thought you were getting your cart back to plain old normal?" He looked over Karl's cart, which still had the bigger tires, stereo speakers, and lights.

"I made them change the stripes and take off a bunch of the bull-crap I don't need," Karl huffed.

"What did they take off?" Jack noticed that only the racing stripes had changed color.

"That damn navigational system! And you don't need one either, just a waste of money!"

Jack leaned in Karl's cart looking at a small led screen mounted to the dash. "What is that?"

"It's a display for the weather and forecast," Karl smiled.

Jack looked at him with a funny expression. "You need an outside display to tell you what the weather is that you're standing in?"

"That's what I told him," Betty spoke up.

"Mind your own damn business," Karl grumbled at Jack. "What are you doing, anyway?"

Jack leaned into his cart, opened his custom wood humidifier, and snatched a couple of Cuban cigars. "I forgot to bring these up." He walked back with Karl and Betty, and when they reached the elevator, Karl stood back, letting Jack punch the up button.

The doors closed, and they rode up one flight, stopping on the second floor. "Oh, good grief," Karl rolled his eyes, guessing who was getting on the elevator. The doors opened to Violet, who was carrying one of her last boxes, and her tired face lit up when she saw Karl. Karl just shook his head and looked up, trying to ignore her, but to his surprise, she remained quiet too.

The elevator stopped on the fifth floor, and as Karl and Betty stepped off, Karl looked back at Jack and Violet, who had grins on their faces as the door shut and they rode one more flight up. "Where in the hell are they going?" Jack asked Betty.

"There's no telling." Betty unlocked their door and disappeared inside, leaving Karl still looking at the elevator. Before the door closed, Karl grabbed it and walked in, stopping by the refrigerator for a glass of milk. He kicked off his shoes and fell back in his recliner, kicking up the foot rest and turning on the TV. As he began flipping through channels, though, a loud bang came from outside. He turned and glanced outside, not seeing anything, then settled back into cursing that nothing was on TV until he came across a western channel.

Betty yelled from the bedroom, "I'm going to go to the restroom."

"Why are you tell me that?" he yelled back. "I don't need to know everything . . . I hope everything comes out OK!" he yelled back with a laugh.

Betty poked her head out of the bedroom. "What was that?" she asked.

"Nothing." He waved her off and pointed at the TV. "John Wayne is on."

Karl took a swig of his milk just as The Duke pulled his pistol and shot a bad guy with the perfect timing of another loud bang outside. Karl muted the channel and listened carefully. "Huh," he said to himself and went back to the show. Another bang! He muted the show and climbed out of his recliner and walked in the bedroom. "You OK?"

"What, honey?" Betty answered him through the bathroom door. Before he could say anything, another bang, this time louder, came from outside. He slid open the balcony door and walked out onto his balcony, still listening carefully.

In the darkness of the late evening, Karl's eyes had just adjusted to the condos on the beach when a bright red explosion of fireworks blinded him just feet off his balcony. After catching his breath, he raced to the railing.

"What in the hell!" he yelled out into the darkness looking for the culprit.

Another loud explosion coming from above him rattled his teeth, sending another red streak across the sky and forming a red and blue firework ball of fire. Karl leaned out the railing and looked up to his worst nightmare, Violet looking down with the same grin she had in the elevator. "Hello Karl!"

"What in Sam Hill are you doing up there?"

Jack leaned over and down at Karl. "Hey, neighbor." Before anyone could say anything else, Karl raced through his apartment, slamming his glass of milk down on the counter. "Honey, what's going on?" Betty asked, walking out of the bathroom, but the only answer she got was the door slamming.

Karl didn't give the elevator a chance and stormed up the stairs located next to the elevator. With no knocking, he burst into the apartment above him, finding it fully furnished and June sitting at the kitchen island. She smiled. "Welcome to our new apartment."

Jack and Violet waiting on the balcony heard his comment—along with the rest of south Alabama. "LIKE HELL YOUR NEW APARTMENT!"

He marched out onto the balcony to find the collection of fireworks Violet had purchased the past summer. "Who let you up here?" he demanded.

Violet lifted one eyebrow. "CBC and a bunch of Benjamin Franklins."

"Did you have something to do with this?" he pointed at Jack.

"It's a free country, plus it'll be fun to have them just above us," Jack answered.

"Fun!?!" Karl's voice shot up to another new record.

Betty walked in the front door to be greeted by June with a hug; they had started to talk when Karl rushed back through the apartment, announcing, "I'm getting the director."

"She's probably gone home for the evening," Betty said in a calm voice.

"Let's go! We'll get a hotel room until the director gets back." Karl stormed out the door.

Betty looked at everyone. "Give him a day or two." The smile came back to her face as she added, "I'm so happy you're just one floor up from us now." She looked at June, who was smiling with her. Jack and Violet went back out onto the balcony to smoke the cigars he had grabbed. Instead of waiting on Betty, Karl rode the elevator down to the lobby and marched to his golf cart, driving off through CBC heading to the beach, blood pressure skyrocketing.

Chapter 50

As the sun peeked over the eastern horizon, Jack set his coffee down on his table and began pulling the advertisements from his paper. Reading the front page, he heard Karl's sliding glass door open and cut his eyes to see Karl coming out onto the balcony. Both nodded toward each other without a word, and after Karl threw his advertisements out, he joined Jack sitting in his chair on his balcony. Both men heard another sliding glass door open and shut, and the twelve inches that separated the two balconies gave Jack enough room to look up and see Violet pull up her chair directly above Karl and settle in with her paper.

She gave Jack a casual salute and began reading her paper. Karl looked over at Jack, asking, "Is she above me?"

"Yep," he answered, staring at his paper.

"Redneck!" He barked just loud enough for Violet to hear.

"Putts," she answered while reading her paper. From a bird's eye view, the threesome sat reading and drinking coffee as if they had never feuded. Betty stood inside staring out the glass door and shaking her head at Karl, who she had worked on calming down most of the evening.

"Ha!" Violet exclaimed loudly, causing both men to look up from their paper.

"Are we going to have to explain the quiet rule to our neighbor?" Karl asked, looking at Jack.

"Read page three," Violet added. Both men turned to page 3 to find a picture of both CBC and the resort next door and the article titled "Seniors Battle for Their Beach Space." All three sank into the article, each secretively racing to finish first.

"Can they take the land?" Karl asked, Jack still reading.

"I don't know, but they have a compelling case," he answered.

"Well, if they take our beach, I'm going to bury thirty pounds of mercury in the sand and then call the EPA. That'll shut the beach down for a year," Violet said from above.

"Where are you going to get thirty pounds of mercury?" Karl set his paper down.

"You'd be surprised," she answered.

Karl picked up his paper, muttering "No. I wouldn't." For the next half hour, the trio sat quietly reading their papers and drinking coffee until Betty broke the silence. "You ready for breakfast?" She opened the door.

Karl looked at Jack. "Twenty minutes?"

"Yep." He pulled himself up from his chair, and both men disappeared into their doors heading to their bathrooms.

Betty walked out onto the balcony. "Would you and June like to join us?" She spoke for Violet to hear.

"Twenty minutes," she heard Violet answer, and then her door shut.

And twenty-one minutes later, the elevator door opened on the fifth floor with June and Violet already inside. Jack, Karl, and Betty also stepped inside. The group slowly strolled to the restaurant with June and Betty leading the way, deep into a conversation about a new store opening down the street. Jack looked down the sidewalk to see Derrick checking out the fountain that was barely spitting out any water, and once Derrick looked up, Jack waved him on for breakfast. They all went through the line picking out something different from each other, with Betty politely shaking her head at everything she was offered until she came to the chocolate pie.

"Keeping it youthful?" Rev. Carter blurted out, seeing her tray with pie and ice tea.

She blushed. "Not so loud."

Laughing, Rev. Carter joined their table, asking, "So how is the Apple-dumpling Gang doing this morning? Heard there was a big move yesterday!"

"You bringing over a welcome gift?" Violet asked. "Is there a gift for removing?" He laughed.

"You can bring the chips for tonight's strip poker game." She took a bite of her eggs.

Rev. Carter started to laugh, then looked at Karl, who answered, "I've yet to lose my underwear." The reverend stopped laughing.

"They're teasing you," June said, patting his arm. "Karl loses his underwear every time." The reverend wasn't sure what to say with no-one laughing or commenting on the subject.

"Good morning." Derrick set his tray down, then looked at Rev. Carter. "How are you this morning?"

"I'm not sure." He looked over at the table at the others, who were all busy eating. Dianna sat down on the other side of him and struck up a conversation with June, causing the table to burst into different subjects.

"She is such a dish!" June spoke up above the conversations, causing everyone to turn and see who she was talking about. Kat gave a simple smile and wave, wondering what they were saying about her. June turned to Derrick. "Go get that girl back! Do you know how hard it was for us to get y'all together? She's your soul mate!"

Derrick smiled. "Working on it."

"Soul mate? You don't believe in soul mates?" Rev. Carter looked at June, who gave him a confused look. "Never mind, of course you do." He went back to drinking his coffee.

June began explaining her healing rocks for soul mates to Rev. Carter when Sylvia Westheimer stormed into the restaurant, searching each table from the door until she spotted Jack, then quickly walked over, "Jack!"

He looked up. "Good morning."

"Come on!" she said and walked back out as quickly as she came in. Jack didn't say anything, but shot up from the table and jogged to catch up with her.

The table watched the commotion until June spoke up. "It's kinda of early for a booty call."

The reverend spit out his coffee. "A what?"

"Booty call. That's what the young people call it," June innocently replied.

"This conversation is deeper than I need to hear. You all have a great morning," Derrick said, standing up. "You have your work cut out for you," he said to Rev. Carter.

Rev. Carter looked up at him. "I'm pretty sure it's too late."

Derrick walked over to the table that Kat was sitting at and pulled up a chair to visit with her while the table was watching them. "Too bad that's not a booty call," June spoke up.

"You do know the Bible says sex out of wedlock is a sin," Rev. Carter said.

Everyone at the table looked at him with a funny expression. "Then you're not coming to our poker game tonight?" Karl devilishly grinned.

Jack and Sylvia entered her small loft apartment and sat in front of the computer screen, "There she is, there!" Sylvia pointed to a social media account.

Jack sat back, saying, "Wow, Delilah."

Chapter 51

"Derrick, I'm sorry, I just don't know how this is going to work," Kat replied, still sitting at the breakfast table.

"It was working fine."

"Was," she answered. Derrick's phone rang and after looking at it, he glanced back up at Kat. "Go work," she said.

Not wanting to leave the conversation, Derrick walked to the door and disappeared into the office on the other end of the call. Kat sat back in her chair watching Derrick walk toward the office in deep thought. "Come on, Kat, stop being so dramatic," she said out loud to herself.

A voice startled her. "I wouldn't call it dramatic. It's hard to give your heart after a traumatic relationship," Betty softly replied.

"Oh, sorry. I didn't know anyone could hear me." She blushed.

"Don't let your mind go crazy. Follow your heart. God sure gave you a beautiful one," Betty said with a smile and followed Karl out.

With her elbows on the table, Kat dropped her face into her hands, watching the Rutherfurds leave the restaurant. Her pocket buzzed with a call, and pulling out her cell phone, she didn't recognize the number. With a reluctant voice she answered.

"Hi, Kat, I hope it's OK to call you. The front desk gave me your number," the voice replied.

"Who is this?"

"Oh, sorry. This is Evan Harriman."

Kat's eyes widened. "Hello, is everything OK?"

"Yeah, yeah. Everything is fine. I was calling not for CBC business, but to ask if you would like to have dinner tonight."

"Oh." Her mind went blank. "It's just dinner," he replied.

"Can I get back to you on that today?" She scrambled for words.

"You can say no."

"No, I need to look at my schedule. I'm eating breakfast right now. I'll text you back in an hour or so."

"OK, I hope it fits in your schedule. Talk to you soon." He hung up. With her head spinning, Kat slowly set the cell phone on the table. "Don't let your mind go crazy," she repeated the words from Betty.

"Talking to yourself?" Violet walked up.

With a half chuckle, Kat replied, "Yea, I guess I am."

"Somedays talking to myself is the best conversation of the day," Violet said and started out.

June stopped at Kat's table. "Where are you going?" she called to Violet.

"Got to meet someone." "Who?"

"Just someone," Violet shouted back, leaving June with Kat. She kept walking toward the Tower lobby, and once entering the lobby doors, said, "Good morning, hope you guys haven't been waiting long?"

The young man that had helped her move stood in the lobby with a beautiful young woman and two small kids. "Nope, we just walked in," he replied.

The young woman stuck out her hand. "Hi, I'm Jena, and these two guys are Dusty and Remington." She pointed to her children.

"Dusty, Remington, I sure like those names." Violet looked back at Jena, "Your husband tells me you're a gun collector too."

With a soft smile, Jena replied, "I am. I told Justin I didn't want to intrude."

"Nonsense, let's head up and I'll show you my collection." She turned back to the boys, who were both under 10, adding, "And maybe we can take the ATV for a spin afterwards." Their faces lit up. The five rode up the elevator to the sixth floor with Justin talking about Violet's wine and putting the racks together.

Violet unlocked her door. "I like to make wine as a hobby, but recently a friend and I have been bootlegging to local stores and restaurants."

"Oh," Jena looked at Justin with a funny expression. "Does that bother you?" Violet asked.

"No, just surprised with the voluntary confession." "At eighty-four years old, everything is voluntary,"

Violet answered. They walked in, the boys running into the living room pointing at the guns that lined the walls and stacked in the corners. Jena eyes grew twice their size, as she couldn't believe the amount of guns in a small apartment.

"And the retirement community doesn't mind you having this many guns?"

"Nah, I give them wine."

Justin waved toward the door leading to the carboys of wine. "Look at this. This is what I was putting together the other day." Justin and Jena disappeared into the room, her mouth wide open in awe.

Violet walked into the living room with the boys, asking, "What kind of guns do you boys like?"

In a shy, high-pitched tone, "I like western guns," one of them answered.

"Six shooters!" Violet opened a cabinet door, exposing a couple of dozen revolvers from nickel-plated Smith and Wessons to pearl-handled Colt 45s. The boys' eyes grew larger just like their mother's, and big smiles formed on their faces.

With the sound of the front door opening, June walked in to see Violet in the living room with the two boys holding a revolver. "Violet?" she asked, still holding the front door open.

"Yea?"

"There are children in here. Why do you have children in here?" she asked. Violet gave her a dirty look and went back to showing the boys the gun. "You're not going to eat them?" she asked.

Both boys looked up at her. "This is Dusty and Remington," Violet explained.

"You've named them?"

The young couple walked out of the wine room. "Hi," Jena said.

June recognized Justin. "Oh, hi. I remember you from helping us move."

"Yes, ma'am, Ms. Violet asked my wife and I back to show us her gun collection. These are our two boys," he added.

June shut the door. "Whew, thank God," she replied, leaving the young couple to question.

Chapter 52

Jaqs walked into her class, which was still a mixture of ladies interested in getting sharp and men who were just interested in Jaqs. "Since it is such a beautiful day, would you guys like to have class on the beach?" A smile formed across the faces of the ladies in the front of the class, while a low grumble formed from the men in the back. "I'll take that as a 'yes' from the majority. Everyone grab a mat and let's walk over to the beach."

Half the class, mostly ladies, grabbed a mat while the other half disbursed into the courtyard and other areas of CBC. With their folded mats under their arms, the ladies marched across the bridge like they were storming the beaches of Normandy. Jaqs followed with a big smile, proud of her class and their enthusiasm for staying in shape.

A low roar came from behind the class, and looking back, Jaqs saw Violet in her ATV with two small children riding shotgun, each wearing a helmet. At the bottom of the stairs Jaqs gave her room to drive by. "Hi, Violet, who are the children?" Jaqs asked, semi-concerned.

Violet shouted, "Supper" before spinning the tires on the sand and throwing a spray of white sand twenty feet behind her. The class watched for a moment as she raced toward the water and turned east, not letting up on the gas. As the class spread out over the sand, Jaqs saw June and the young couple top over the bridge, giving her a little comfort about Violet and kids. With the walk wiping out over half the class, Jaqs went light on the class, going for only 20 minutes. Just as she was about to finish, one of the ladies made the comment about the snotty suit walking their way. Jaqs looked at Hank, giving him a gesture that she'd be through in a minute.

"I hope he isn't going to try to run us off," one of the ladies said.

"No, I wouldn't let him do that," Jaqs answered and walked over to him.

June watched on with a concerned expression, wondering why Jaqs was talking to him and worried her sister would return with Hank still on the beach. It was just his luck that a silhouette of an ATV formed from down the beach. The young couple watched as their children were having a great time in the ATV, oblivious of everyone else's thoughts for the safety of Hank, still standing on the beach.

Violet stopped shy of the parking area for CBC and switched seats with one of the children. With the other child seated in her lap, Violet said something that couldn't be heard over the engine and pointed toward Hank. With tires spinning, the rear end of the ATV sinking in the sand, and smoke pouring out of the mufflers, the side by side shot out of its stance toward Jaqs and Hank. Jaqs threw up her arms and dove toward June and the young couple while Hank took shelter on top a container box that housed the resort chairs and umbrellas.

After a couple of donuts in the sand, the ATV came to a rest beside the container box. "Sorry, Hank, little man here has a heavy foot," Violet said, helping the kids take off their helmets.

"I'm sure." He hesitantly climbed down from the box with Violet and one of the boys climbing out of the ATV. Landing on the sand and still facing the box, Violet grabbed both sides of his waist and yelled, "Vroom! Watch out!"

Hank squealed like a four-year-old girl, "Don't touch me!"

Violet turned to the little boy, who was still sitting in her ATV, explaining, "That's what happens to your voice if you don't eat your vegetables." Both kids laughed.

June and the young couple walked up, helping the one boy out of the side by side while Jaqs helped Hank dust off. "I see you two are getting acquainted," June replied.

"Just friends," he answered, straightening his jacket. "Uh huh." June cocked one side of her mouth.

Hank motioned for Jaqs to follow him back to the

resort, and Violet and June walked with the young couple and the kids to the water. As they were playing in the water, Kat walked over the bridge, noticing Jaqs disappear into the resort front doors.

"I just passed Jaqs' class going into the fitness center; was that Jaqs going into the resort?" Kat asked June, walking up to the group.

"Yep. Looks kinda fishy."

Kat looked back. "I'd say so." She pointed to the couple and kids.

June smiled. "Violet's new friends. I have to head back, so why don't you walk with me?" she asked Kat.

Kat gave a friendly wave and headed back with June, walking together. They stopped for a brief moment on top of the bridge and looked back at Violet. "I think her grandmother instincts are setting in," June said.

"Violet?"

June laughed. "Yep, even that old biddy has a heart." They were continuing their trek back to the main campus of CBC when a figure appeared on the walk several feet in front of them.

"Dang," Kat replied.

"I take it you're not interested in Gerald's grandson." "No, and I don't have a clue how to turn him down for a date."

"If you scratch your crotch and say something about a rash, that'll normally run them off," June grinned.

Kat laughed. "I think I'll save that for another time." She walked toward Evan to break any possibilities of a date.

Chapter 53

Hank opened his office door and looked back at his secretary. "I'm not to be bothered," he instructed her, following Jaqs in and shutting the door. A smile formed on his face. "I have met with a few investors who are interested in buying the resort."

"Really?" Jaqs straightened up.

"And once the deal is done, you are looking at the new CEO."

"Really?" Her tone changed, and she took a step closer to him.

He placed his arm around her waist. "So, do you want to come run the fitness center at one of the most prestigious resorts on the coast in Alabama?"

"I don't know, maybe," she teased him, running her fingers through his hair.

"What can I do to persuade you?" he asked with their lips inches apart.

"There's a call on line 1," a voice came over the phone intercom.

Hank pressed the button. "I said no interruptions." "Sorry to interrupt your hanky-panky time, but the caller said it's urgent."

He pushed Jaqs off him. "The first thing to go is that old bat!" He picked up the phone, "Hello!" Jaqs watched his face turn from angry to concerned. "What do you mean, the court time was cancelled? When are we rescheduling? I want that piece of beach property!" He slammed the phone down.

"What's wrong?" Jaqs asked.

"I don't know. They cancelled the court time." He stormed to the door. "Come on, we are going to go find out why CBC is playing games!" He marched out, followed by Jaqs in a prissy jog.

Next door, June watched from a distance as Kat spoke with Evan on what she thought was a broken date, but instead was a conversation about Evan calling an emergency meeting with board members, the director, Derrick, and Kat.

As the members arrived, Derrick walked up, seeing Kat and Evan standing outside talking, and before he reached them, Kat walked inside, leaving the two men outside. "I know you're pursuing Kat, and money to money I can't match you, but it will—"

Evan held up his hand, cutting Derrick off. "Save your breath. I did ask Kat out since you two were not seeing each other, but she just said 'no' to me." Evan looked at him. "You need to capitalize on that before I have time to rethink my strategy on asking her out." He held the door open for Derrick, who remained speechless.

Evan and Derrick walked in to find everyone standing in the foyer talking, and three seconds later the door exploded with Hank and Jaqs marching in. "What in the hell are you people pulling?" Hank screamed. "You can try and hold this in the courts as long as you want— we'll still use all the beach space!"

The director looked at Jaqs. "Why are you with Hank?"

"I'm going to be his new fitness instructor once he buys the resort," she proudly announced.

Hank frantically waved his hands toward her. "Shhh! That's not to be known." Everyone in the room became quiet hearing the news, and fear started to loom in the room about the emergency meeting. "But now that it's out," he glanced at Jaqs, "yes I am buying the resort!"

"Let's take this into the board room," Evan suggested.

Entering the board room and before everyone could get in their seats, one of the directors asked, "Evan, is this what the meeting is about? Did someone else buy the resort?"

Evan and Hank locked eyes. "Well, to be honest, Evan replied, I wasn't aware when we first met that someone was interested in buying the resort." Hank sat up with a smile on his face. "And just recently I learned of a group of investors wanting to make an offer and put Hank in the CEO seat."

"So, things will be changing soon and we will be taking the beach space that is owed to us," Hank smiled, leaving the board members in an array of disbelief.

"But!" Evan looked at Hank. "I just signed the papers this morning taking one hundred percent of the ownership of the resort," Evan added, followed by a relieved gasp from the members.

Hank's face froze with his smile still plastered on it, and Jaqs turned to him. "What does this mean?" she asked with no response from him.

"It means that if you want a job at the resort as a fitness instructor, you'll be working for CBC. I have incorporated the two into one entity," Evan explained.

Hank made a funny noise, still frozen. "So we own all the beach space now," Kat spoke up first.

Evan smiled, "Yes."

The funny noise from Hank got louder. "I would like to ask the board to make a motion for the CBC director to take a new role as executive director over both properties," Evan continued.

"Are you good with that?" one of the board members asked her.

"Yes," she answered. "With the notation that Derrick becomes the permanent director over CBC."

"Absolutely!" the member answered her. "Let's call this meeting into order."

The director turned to Hank. "Hank? As your new boss, you are dismissed from the meeting. I'll be over to discuss your role as assistant manager." He made another funny noise with a nod and quickly exited the building like a dog with its tail tucked. The director looked at Jaqs. "I noticed the fitness center is in disarray. You need to head over there and clean it up; we have high standards here at CBC."

"Huh!" Jaqs flipped her hair and walked out.

The director stood up from her chair. "I guess I need to give you your chair." She smiled at Derrick.

Chapter 54

Kat smiled at Derrick as he slid into his new chair and role at CBC, followed by a round of applause from the board members. Clapping, Kat felt her phone buzz with a text from Jack. "I need to see you." "Ok, give me just a few minutes." She slipped it back in her pocket.

"I'm afraid I don't have a few minutes," he replied. "Kat, please stay with us," the director said, seeing Kat heading toward the door.

Kat looked at Derrick and Evan, then put her phone back in her pocket with a strange expression. "I would like to, but Jack is texting me. Let me go check on him."

Kat left the offices texting Jack back to let him know she was walking over. What do you mean you don't have a minute? Bad thoughts entered her head. Her walk turned into a small jog that picked up into a dead run as she entered the lobby of The Towers. Once at his front door she knocked, and not hearing anyone or movement from inside, she knocked harder and loud enough for the entire floor to hear. Still not hearing any response, she turned the door knob, finding it unlocked, and froze in the doorway once the door swung open.

Jack walked in from his balcony dressed in his white slacks, bowling style shirt, and fedora hat. His apartment cleaned, all the lights off, and two packed bags in the kitchen. "Jack? You scared the crap out of me with your text. What's the matter? Are you going somewhere?"

He held out his hand. "Let's talk on the balcony." He held her hand. And once back on the balcony, he went on, "Kat, years are short and spending them with the right people is important."

Her heart was still racing. "What's the matter? You're scaring me."

Jack chuckled. "I don't mean to. Listen, kiddo, I have lived my life trying to buy love as a blind man. The first gal I ever fell in love with took my heart, and I aim to go get her!"

"Delilah?"

"Sylvia has been helping me locate her on social media."

"Sylvia? I thought you two—"

Laughing, "No, no. Sylvia is definitely a catch, but not for me. I just let you guys think that for fun." He tightened his grip. "Stop fooling around and give yourself to Derrick. He's by far the best catch!"

She smiled. "He is."

"Good! Then you'll talk with him today?"

"OK?" She wasn't sure why, but tears starting forming in her eyes. "Where are you going, and when are you coming back?"

"Help me with my bags." They walked out together. "New York, and I don't know."

"Have you told Karl?" "Nah, he gets all sappy."

"Jack! You need to tell him," she said.

He smiled. "Tell him for me. I'm not good at goodbyes."

They walked out of the lobby to a waiting taxi. "Take care of my golf cart." He handed her the keys.

Tears starting falling. "You better come back!"

He kissed her on her cheek. "You will always be the daughter I always wanted." He sat in the back of the cab and looked at the driver in the rearview mirror. "To the airport, please." He looked at Kat and smiled with one last wink.

As the cab disappeared around the corner of the Tower Apartments, Kat texted Derrick, "Are you still in the meeting?"

She stood in the drive waiting his reply. "No, it was a fast meeting. I am walking out to the beach trying to wrap my head around this. A lot of stuff fast," he texted back.

"Can we talk?" "Of course."

Kat thought for a moment of walking to the bridge,

but then looked down at Jack's keys in her hand. She smiled walking toward his cart. As she drove through the property of CBC, everyone waved, not thinking anything of Kat driving Jack's cart. She topped the bridge looking out over the beach, only seeing one person.

Derrick.

Parking the cart, she slipped out of her shoes to allow her toes to sink in the white sand. A warm breeze blew her hair back out of her face and with each step, her feet made a squeaky noise against the sand. Derrick stood near the water facing her, their eyes locked, and as if they had never quarreled, they both smiled.

"Congratulations," she said as she approached him. "Thanks. Crazy day." Taking a chance, he reached out for her hand.

They locked fingers and walked toward the water. Standing in the sand facing the gulf, she grinned. "So it's safe to say that I'm dating my boss?"

"I don't like the way that sounds," he answered. "Well, it's true with you as the director now." "The dating part."

"What do you mean?" She looked at him, puzzled, as he stepped back. Kat started to say something else, but stopped when Derrick fell to one knee, holding out a small navy blue box.

About the Author

 Lee DuCote has traveled researching cultures, people, and historical accounts to help create his stories. A native to Louisiana, he writes to give hope and encouragement to others, as well as to entertain and spark the imagination. Lee lives in the Ozark Mountains of Arkansas with his wife and family and is the author of *Fields of Alicia*, *Waterproof*, and *Across Borders*. You can visit him and see more or follow him at the links below:

Connect with Lee DuCote

 www.leeducote.com    @leeducote

 @leeducote    www.faccbook.com/authorleeducot